BOY INTO PANTHER
AND OTHER STORIES

BOY INTO PANTHER
AND OTHER STORIES

by Margaret Benbow

Many Voices Project
#135

©2017 by Margaret Benbow
First Edition
Library of Congress Control Number: 2016959983
ISBN: 978-0-89823-357-5
e-ISBN: 978-0-89823-358-2

Cover and interior design by Brittany Schultz
Author photo by Deborah Max Reisman

The publication of *Boy Into Panther And Other Stories* is made possible by the generous support of Minnesota State University Moorhead, the Dawson Family Endowment, and other contributors to New Rivers Press.

MINNESOTA STATE UNIVERSITY MOORHEAD.   THE MᶜKNIGHT FOUNDATION

For copyright permission, please contact Frederick T. Courtwright at 570-839-7477 or permdude@eclipse.net.

New Rivers Press is a nonprofit literary press associated
with Minnesota State University Moorhead.

Nayt Rundquist, Managing Editor
Kevin Carollo, Editor, MVP Poetry Coordinator
Travis Dolence, Director
George McCormack, MVP Prose Coordinator
Thomas Anstadt, Co-Art Director
Trista Conzemius, Co-Art Director
Thom Tammaro, Poetry Editor
Alan Davis, Editor Emeritus

Publishing Interns:
Laura Grimm, Anna Landsverk, Mikaila Norman

Boy Into Panther and Other Stories book team:
Alyssa Amstrup, Wyatt Feten, Kaitlin Laither, Samuel Rude

∞ Printed in the USA on acid-free, archival-grade paper.

Boy Into Panther And Other Stories is distributed nationally
by Small Press Distribution.

New Rivers Press
c/o MSUM
1104 7th Ave S
Moorhead, MN 56563
www.newriverspress.com

For my family

"I like reality. It tastes of bread."
—Jean Anouilh

CONTENTS

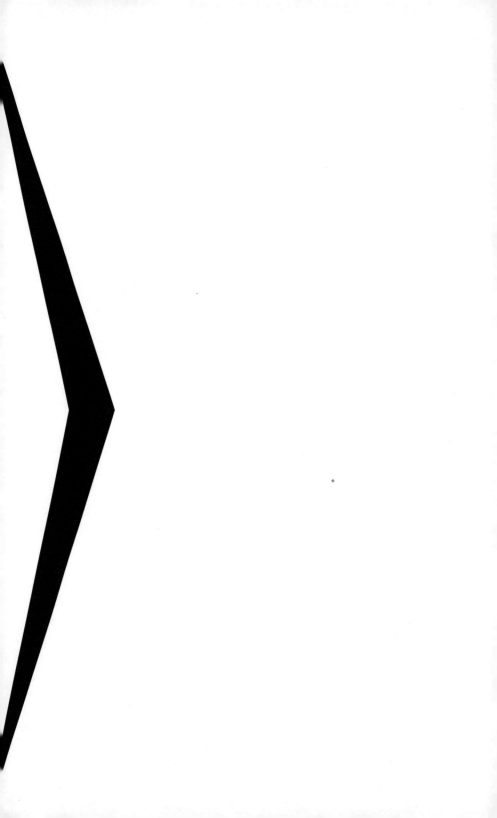

BOY INTO PANTHER

The first time Consolata saw Carlo Puovi, he was kneeling on Ambrose Reilly's chest, clutching the hair of the much bigger boy in both fists and pounding his head against the cement of the schoolyard. In the same instant, Father Karl Dubroski came running out of the church shouting to Carlo in his horrible Spanish: *You are in America now. You are here now. Not every fight has to be to the death.*

Father Karl did his best to wrench Carlo off Ambrose, but the boy did not want to let go and fastened himself to Ambrose like a raptor with razor talons and beak. In the end, Father Karl had to half stifle Carlo in his own enormous black coat, bag him like a rabid dog, and haul him upside down in a fireman's hold into the school. Carlo first saw Consolata from this position. He looked with curiosity at the pretty girl standing quietly among her hysterical schoolmates in her unspotted white dress, and she returned his gaze calmly. His upended head kept bouncing against Father Karl's backside as the priest plunged across the schoolyard, and involuntarily she smiled. With his eyes on hers, Carlo raised his fists, opened them, and released Ambrose's red curls into the wind with a formal gesture of blessing.

The Puovis were refugees from an incredibly isolated and primitive province in South America, so far back, and so deep in, that nobody at St. Rita's Parochial School had even heard its name. Sister Ursula did show her class a map of this province, and it looked like an attacking black panther with blue rivers of entrails. Sister Ursula explained to Consolata and others in the sixth grade that, although this province was the poorest, most godforsaken place on the face of the earth, the inhabitants were fighting over it in a civil war. The Puovi family had been trapped between the different factions and had had many unfortunate experiences. It was a miracle, and due entirely to God's grace, that in the end they escaped with their lives. Everyone in the class should thank God, and be kind to poor little Carlo. This was before they had actually seen him.

Privately, Sister Ursula pondered the few words Carlo's mother had said to her when she enrolled her children at St. Rita's. Mrs. Puovi explained in her bizarre English that because her husband was a dreamer, it was Carlo, her oldest son, who planned and led the escape from the civil war. The mother seemed to add that Carlo had had to kill a few soldiers, but the teacher decided that she must not have heard her right.

Carlo's parents never lost the look of battered and terrified stowaways, people born to live in small, malodorous spaces like caves, cells, or anchor holds. All of the younger Puovis suffered from a variety of disgusting ailments—worms, chiggers, lice— and Carlo himself had rat bites on his legs. The school nurse dosed and physicked them savagely for months.

Carlo looked very different from the rest of the family. If a human female had lain with an alpha wolf and conceived, the result might have looked like Carlo. He had eyes of a silvery grey, like a virulently alive ghost, and stiff black hair so vigorous no cap could contain it. His features were the proudest of crags. His shoulders filled doorways and burst through the tragic steerage pullovers his mother bought for him. He wore shoes that a good horse would have disdained, but he won every race.

When Carlo first came to St. Rita's, although he was twelve years old, he had never brushed his teeth in his life. He didn't speak a word of English. When the others were studying, Sister Ursula would give him colored pencils and paper. She didn't know what else to do with him. The first day, he drew highly detailed pictures of sumptuous grapes and cherries, which he'd seen in Consolata's lunch, and of soldiers burning houses down. The second day, he drew oranges and apples, and himself cutting a soldier's head off with a machete. Sister Ursula had no idea how to respond to this work, of which he seemed quite proud.

He learned to read, write, and speak English much more quickly than Sister Ursula had expected. At first he read as though he were translating ancient hieroglyphics and wrote as though he were inscribing them. Because of this, other students sometimes made fun of him. But the same person never made fun of him twice.

Sister Ursula did not like surprises of any kind, and so she studied some of his homework and exams—particularly in math and English—with a frown. How could he understand this? Could he be cheating? Then she would look at his other work, in civics and religion, and her brow would clear. It was as she had foretold. The boy was a dunce.

A flu epidemic almost emptied the eighth-grade classroom the spring that Carlo and Consolata were fourteen. They ate lunch together every day for three weeks. Consolata was an only child, and her tender little sandwiches were the only ones in the school that were innocent of crusts. They were filled with tiny cubes of egg salad, shaved chicken breast, and tuna with the dark parts cut out. Her tomatoes were seeded, and she ate with a monogrammed silver spoon.

"Your peaceful little lunches," Carlo said. He in his turn hauled out a crushed and greasy bag, often foul-smelling from some unspeakable leak. She tried not to look at his savage lunches, but sometimes took a peek. Animal body parts that resembled shattered hunks of liver, heart, or raw brawn—she hardly knew which, but they made the filthy waxed paper wet and red—drooled into the whole onions, often complete with their muddy roots. She had seen Mrs. Puovi pawing through the dead-vegetable bin at the market, and fully believed the rank, tangled objects in the bottom of the bag could be anything at all—hair balls, livid orange fungi, shriveled garlic bulbs, toe-

nails. It was well-known that Mrs. Puovi had suffered a great
deal in the civil war, and was not in her right mind. Carlo ate
through these crazed lunches stolidly, with every appearance
of satisfaction.

At first, they were almost silent as they ate. One day, however, Mrs. Blanca y Blanca had made a particularly perfect lunch
for her daughter. Carlo couldn't take his eyes off it. He thought
it was as though the mother were making an offering of var-
ied, exquisite ambrosias to her baby goddess. Even the deviled
egg fascinated him, its finely sieved yolk planted with a slice of
stuffed olive. Consolata herself was as self-contained as an egg,
and the moment came when he couldn't stand it any longer. He
picked up her little golden banana and casually stuck it in his ear.
Yawning, he stuffed raspberries in his nostrils. He seized the egg
and clapped it to his upper cheek, where it stuck. He expected
Consolata to scream for the nuns at the sight of the mashed, hel-
lacious devil eye sliding down his face, but she surprised him by
laughing. In fact, in a girl less pretty, it would have been called a
belly laugh. After that, they talked all lunch hour. They discussed
the beating Father Karl had given Ambrose Reilly for insolence
that morning, a beating so savage and protracted that, in the end,
the boy had to be carried home by his parents. Carlo said he
had always suspected Father Karl suffered from lurid patholo-
gies, and this proved it. Consolata thought about this in her calm
way for a moment or two, and then said politely but very firmly,
"Ambrose was insolent. We should remember that Father Karl
was not really beating Ambrose, but the devil in Ambrose."

Consolata was surprised when her friends said Carlo was
frighteningly ugly, crude, and incoherent. She privately thought
that he looked like a picture she'd seen of the great Incan ruler
Manco Cápac. His eyes blazed out the same way. Of course,
you had to forget his terrible clothes. As for his conversation, he
made perfect sense to her.

During these weeks, they had only one brief argument. One
day Carlo had in his lunch what appeared to be a boiled dog

jowl and a half-rotten plantain. He became annoyed at the finicky gestures with which Consolata ate her darling little lunch. She took tiny bites of her pudding, fairy sips from the lemonade bottle. Something about the way she searched out strawberry seeds from the corners of her lush lips with a snowy napkin particularly maddened him.

"You little *burro* princess!" he said, using the word with which South Americans of Indian descent dryly tease and identify each other. She turned pale with outrage.

"I am not an Indian," she said. "My family is pure Spanish. My mother told me so."

Now, Carlo had seen Mrs. Blanca y Blanca at the market, haughtily rejecting black grapes. She looked like the Indian on the Big Chief writing pads, and her skin was a proud shining copper. When Consolata said she was pure Spanish, he smiled to himself. However, he said nothing.

Privately, everyone agreed that Carlo's parents were incredibly ignorant and smelly.

"It is because of what they have gone through," Consolata said.

The father's appearance, not to mention his barbaric English, made it difficult for him to find work. However, in time he was befriended by the Communist who lived on his block. The Communist, whose name was Tom, found work for him on a construction site.

Joaquin Puovi was very grateful to his friend for this job, and insisted that Carlo, who was then sixteen, go with him to thank Tom. However, Carlo stayed in Tom's living room only an instant. He stood looking at certain objects and at the numerous pictures on the walls that showed horrible historic events. When Tom explained that he found them fascinating and inspirational, Carlo simply turned and walked out. Joaquin caught up with him a block away, breathless with anger. "What is the matter with you? We owe him everything."

"We owe him nothing. You work hard, you deserve that job. I am not going to converse with a man who keeps a model of Hitler's bunker on top of his TV. He has a picture over the fruit bowl of Mussolini's corpse hanging by its heels from a lamppost. You should stop going there."

"You said once that communists deserve respect—"

"He is not like other communists. He is dangerous. He watches you as an eagle eyes a piece of meat. He has some kind of plan. You are putting yourself at the mercy of a dangerous fool."

But Joaquin returned to his friend's house. That evening, Tom said that the time had come for Joaquin to learn certain tragic truths about the Catholic church. Surely he was aware, or would be as soon as he had the facts, that the church was a bloody abomination that fed on poor men's lives. Had the priests in Joaquin's country helped him during the civil war? Was he aware that the church had supported the most vicious faction of soldiers? When he called on the saints, had they rescued his family? Tom talked like this for hours that night and many nights to come.

Slowly, hatred of the church grew in Joaquin's heart like a blazing particular star. He would walk into the sanctuary at St. Rita's and gaze slowly from face to face of the twenty or more religious statues that, preening in their niches, looked down on his struggles. The more warlike saints glared belligerently about them with a fiery martial air. Others, like Saint Sebastian, with arrows through his temples, palms, and heart, wept and bled beads of wood. Statues of the Virgin were often enriched with gold leaf, her dark face surrounded with flowerets and cascades of lace carved from ash and oak boles. Some men had spent their entire working lives, he knew, wrenching carved lace for saints, with tears and with blood, from the hardest materials.

Sweet and pleasant things flowed to these huge, sacred dolls. Flowers clustered around their niches. The stone toe of Saint Jude, patron of impossible causes, was worn smooth by the desperate kisses of the faithful. Mrs. Puovi used to pray to Saint Jude during the civil war.

The time came when, after a long conversation with Tom, Joaquin Puovi decided to blow up the statues. He brought a ladder into the sanctuary late at night, when it was empty, and painstakingly collected all the stone, wood, metal, laced, and jeweled figures. He did not throw them in a heap, but positioned them with an odd dignity, on their feet when possible, in a group before the altar. He then lit the fuse to a bomb in their midst. However, the fuse exploded prematurely, killing Joaquin.

Carlo was the first person in the church after the explosion. He had found out about the scheme, too late, from his mother. His first startled impression, when he saw the richly robed and suavely smiling statues in their ranks and his father's remains dangling from the chandelier, was that aristocrats of iron had somehow conspired to murder the peasant who defied them.

Consolata at fifteen was already famous for knowing the right thing to say on every occasion. Also, she was one of the few students who spoke to Carlo Puovi. "That Consolata Blanca y Blanca, she is so good," said Sister Ursula. "She never gives up, even on the blackest sheep." However, even Consolata did not know how to comfort the son of a deceased, deranged, and unsuccessful terrorist. Besides, Carlo was stoical.

"I found a bomb-making booklet in my father's lunch box," he said. "The Communist gave it to him. He should have known the old fool couldn't read. The Communist is responsible."

And the saints, he added in his own mind.

Behind her back, Sister Ursula's students called her the B.V.M., Black Veiled Monster. However, she had a romantic and even poetic streak that would come out at arbitrary moments. She would suddenly drop the math lesson and begin telling stories of ancient myths with such color and conviction that her students could see Apollo's beast-scowl of rage and frustrated love, hear his howl as Daphne's delicate body grew into the bay tree. On certain days in May, Sister Ursula would seize her Bible and read at length from the meatier passages in the Song of Solomon. She had a deep, beautiful voice, and as she read she noticed that Carlo Puovi listened with a quietness that was unusual for him.

> *Thou art all fair, my love; there is no spot in thee. Come with me from Lebanon, my spouse, with me from Lebanon . . . from the lions' dens, from the mountains of the leopards.*

Sister Ursula would also read from Isaiah, which, she told her students, was actually a great love poem to God. "Look what he says here: 'I have graven thee on the palms of my hands.'" She read, raising her two big hands and opening them to her students, with an ecstatic expression. Stirred by her emotion, they peered closely at her palms and fancied they could see the outline of a divine commanding eye, the curl of a sacred beard.

Consolata's storm system of black hair was untamable, no matter how her mother labored over it with comb, brush, and pomade. Still, at sixteen she wore her hair down her back and dressed in the Virgin's colors, unlike other girls in the tenth grade. When Sister Ursula lifted her great inquisitor's brow to heaven and prayed in the classroom, Consolata screwed up her own eyes so tightly that her brows furrowed. She would also sometimes cover her eyes with a graceful hand during Mass, symbolically shutting out the distractions of the wide and dirty world. Sister Ursula was given to forecasting pious fates for the students she approved of, and she would sometimes put her hand gently on Consolata's wild black mane and say softly, "And there are some whom God blesses by allowing them to braid Saint Catherine's tresses all their lives." Everybody understood that Sister Ursula was tactfully suggesting that Consolata follow in the steps of the virgin martyr—short, of course, of being tortured on the wheel—and enjoy her virginity all her life.

When Carlo saw this, he wanted to laugh wildly. He also wanted to kiss Consolata tenderly, and shake her until her big pearl teeth rattled. Her entire person was like a barbaric gift, which she would have died rather than bestow. But what is a gift for, except to give?

Carlo dared to express this thought to Juan Maera, a former classmate, a cripple, who had his own newspaper stand. Juan, who had been St. Rita's prize student before his father was murdered and he had to quit school, laughed heartily. "It's a gift all right, but only for the right person. You have the wrong voice, the wrong skin, the wrong hair, the wrong mother, father, grandmother, grandfather, all the way back to your rock-dumb, gorilla-hairy old aboriginal ancestors. Even in Incan times, Puovis weren't the high priests in the temple, having fun harvesting human organs for the sacrifices. No. They were the sorry-ass burros laid out on the slab, having their miserable slave hearts cut out. Not much has changed, either."

There was a pause. Then Carlo said in a cold voice, "You're lucky you're already crippled. Give me the fucking newspaper."

When he turned seventeen, Carlo was expelled from St. Rita's almost as a matter of course. Sister Ursula felt a faint twinge, because of his math scores. She knew that he was a brilliant natural mathematician. She had known it all through his high school career. If it had been anyone else, she would have arranged the best private tutors, and later she would have been shaking down the richer members of the congregation, finding scholarships. But, she told herself, anybody could tell by a single look that Carlo Puovi would come to nothing and worse than nothing. She couldn't stand his caste and type. She didn't even like the color of his eyes. Why had he stayed so long at St. Rita's, anyway? Why did he force his way into the Catholic Youth dances every Friday night? He was always thrown out. He was thrown out drunk, kicking at the priests with his snakeskin boots. He was back in black the very next Friday, high on mescaline, dancing brilliantly with back flips, splits, and blazing knee-drops before he was thrown out by the muscular and ferocious Father Karl. In fact, Carlo and Father Karl battled each other every Friday night until both were bleeding from the ears and mouth.

It was a matter of pride for Father Karl to deal with St. Rita's young thugs himself, not to call the police.

Consolata, wearing her everlasting blue and white, would dance with quiet Jaime Perfidia and watch these battles over his shoulder. If she was sitting with friends, the bloody denouement of Carlo's fights often took place directly in front of her folding chair. This happened so often that one of her friends said, "It's as though he is a *torero*, and he pushes his *paseos* right in your face." Except for the hours Carlo spent at the dances Friday nights, no one could be exactly sure where he went or what he was doing during that period. He would often be mysteriously absent for days at a time, and when he returned, he would have money.

The night of Carlo's eighteenth birthday, he showed up in new, narrow black pants, a black shirt poured over his bulging shoulders, and a bolo tie whose clasp consisted of an amethyst the size of a duck egg. Somewhere he had found scented grease with incredible fixative powers, so that his black wolf's hair lay welded to his head in hard scrolls. He spent the evening snaking back and forth in front of Consolata in agonizingly slow, stylized dance steps, with a very beautiful, wild-looking Indian girl, the one whose name was Mesalia, plastered to his front. This girl had come from Carlo's home province. Tightly clasped in each other's arms, the two of them laughed and talked in a strange, guttural dialect that Consolata could not understand.

Several times during the evening Consolata accepted quiet Jaime Perfidia's invitation to dance.

After two hours, Carlo fought with Father Karl and was thrown out. The Indian girl vanished at the same time. Consolata danced with Jaime. She would have said that she was feeling nothing in particular, but after a few minutes she was astonished to find tears on her cheeks. She excused herself, and walked out of the gymnasium where the dance was being held. She walked up to the entrance doors, and then stopped. Through the doors, she could see Carlo standing alone on the sidewalk in front of the school, facing it. He did not look as though he particularly wanted to be there, but he also looked as though no force whatever could tear him away. He just stood on the sidewalk and waited. The night wind had torn his black hair free of the comb tracks of grease he had applied earlier.

Consolata went straight down the school steps to Carlo and took his hand. Without a word they began walking in the direction of the huge park, where her mother had told her never to go. They moved through broad sheaves of moonlight and wind that smelled of black locust. After they reached the park, they crossed a meadow where there were flowers she had not known existed in the city. Here and there she saw dark, flickering figures, lying behind bushes or running in the distance, but she was safe because she was with Carlo.

At last they reached the center of the park: very far back, and very deep in. In the moonlight Consolata could see his dark head and silver eyes, and the black clothes that fit so well she might have shaped them over his body with her own tender hands.

"In the province where I come from," he said, "the groom kidnaps the bride."

She knew that this was actually a question, one that put her whole life in his hands. She nodded with a grave expression that made him smile. He began taking off her white and blue garments one by one. It took him awhile, because he was trying to control the trembling of his hands. At last she stood in the moonlight wearing only her saints' medals, with the great mass of her hair stirring around her. Carlo was so astonished by the beauty of her body that he forgot, for a moment, what it was he had wanted to do. Then he put his hand on her breast and moved it slowly to show her how the nipple stood up on the roselike areola. "Little flower," he said softly.

She stared at his dark hand, and at his smile, which she saw as mocking. She backed away from him with a white face and white teeth clenched like a wolf's. She picked up her white and blue garments. He said, "Consolata," and when she ignored him, in a panic he put his hands on her shoulders.

She wrenched herself free. "Don't touch me," she said. *You dirty Indian* was what he heard. Then she simply walked away from him, into the trees. For a few seconds he could see her body glimmering through the branches, and then she disappeared. As he stood in the clearing he saw his life as it would be, and it coldly watched him, too.

When Consolata walked into the hall at St. Rita's, perfectly groomed as always, the dance had ended. Jaime Perfidia stood waiting for her, holding her coat, an expression of mild bemusement on his handsome features.

Five hours later that night, Carlo put his valise in the front pew and looked up at the wood, metal, and stone faces gleaming in the sanctuary. There they all were, happy way up high. He got the ladder and began work at once. He lifted them down and carried them for what seemed a long time. It was amazing how heavy some of them were. He had to transport Saint Benedict in a fireman's hold. He thought that this particular statue of the saint should be declared patron of the fat instead of the dying. Other statues felt light and fragile, their wooden bones like bundles of twigs for the burning. Saint Barbara, who was invoked against lightning and sudden death, could be lifted as though she were a baby. Calmly he began disassembling the Holy Family.

Carlo did not usually think in metaphors and fables, but he hadn't slept well the night before and was working in a coma of fatigue. It seemed to him that in the past years he had been dreaming in red. He'd been kicked awake and now came to do a work of black. If Father Karl's sermons were correct, he would be towing this darkness behind him for the rest of his life. Well, he could do that. It would be worth it. Still, he remembered Father Karl sticking his huge nose, like a great Polski pickle, over the lectern as he glared at his students and snarled out, "All of your lives you will be choosing between poison and food.

Choose food." Carlo wondered what food worked in that old dragon's gut and brain, nourishing the monster within. What food made him batter the young, assign medieval penances to the old, run mad at dances?

As he worked, Carlo also remembered folktales Sister Ursula used to tell her class. She may have been an evil hag, but she could tell a story. There was one about a Sioux boy who escaped his enemies by turning into a panther. Sister Ursula displayed a picture of a shaman's mask that showed this transformation. A terrible black fell of hair grew in writhing waves over the human features. His nostrils burned red. Ferocious eyebrows of black fur engulfed the sad, clear eyes.

The Sioux boy was hated by many. "He was full of enemies," Sister Ursula said, "as dead meat is of maggots." But this boy had a totem spirit who transplanted cells from a panther's legs into the boy's legs. All around him burned the enemies' fire-glow. From a stone-cold, standing start he leaped gigantically over their astonished faces.

At first, Carlo had planned to arrange the statues in a group before the altar, as his father had done. Upon reflection, he changed his mind and put all but two before the Communion rail. They could not kneel, but at least they would be down where the common folk were, just this once.

The two remaining statues were saints renowned for being virgin martyrs. He thought it was a very Catholic concept: to be revered for experiences one had never had. He arranged these brides of Christ like cordwood on the big cooling board of the altar. Saint Cecilia had a smooth little face, painted in airy pastels like an Easter egg. Saint Apollonia had white flowers growing out of her mouth. Carlo fumbled in his wallet and produced Consolata's most recent class picture, which he had extorted from Jaime Perfidia with menaces the week before. He'd bought a tiny frame for the picture, silvery metal chased with flowers. Consolata looked as though she had been scrubbed, burnished, and all but waxed by her mother, but nothing could really tame that hair. Carlo passed his thumb, once, over the black curls, then carefully placed the picture in Saint Cecilia's palm.

He figured it would take Consolata's mother about three months to marry her off to that nun's-pet eunuch, Jaime Perfidia. Mrs. Blanca y Blanca would have the grand triumphal fantasia of a wedding she'd been plotting for eighteen years. However, he would not see it. He would not be there. He did have one successful relative, an uncle who worked out of Cleveland. He'd decided to stay with the old cutthroat and learn what he had to teach.

The sticks of dynamite. The fuse. He glanced behind him to make sure the escape route was clear. He carried the valise to the church door, then returned to the sanctuary. As he passed the Communion rail, his eye fell on Saint Rita. She wore a crown of roses but held ready a crown of thorns. Oh, that was it. That was the way to be. Desolation, happiness, it was all the same to her. She was prepared, no matter what occurred. He hesitated, then, with something like a smile, lifted and carried the patroness of desperate cases to a place of safety, beside the front entrance.

He returned to the sanctuary. He lit the fuse, and began walking calmly to the exit. At the last instant, as he reached the door, he suddenly turned, rushed all the way back to Saint Cecilia, snatched Consolata's picture from her palm, wheeled again as the fuse hissed against the dynamite, dug for his life and then leaped in an impossibly long vault as the roar and flames blew out every window in the church and filled the air with flying saints' heads and limbs.

Minutes later, he awoke to find himself on the floor at the back of the church. Blazing clouds made up of shimmering red dust and fire dazzled his eyes. Looking down, he could see the picture still clenched in his fist—but was it a life grip or a death grip? He opened his hand and saw that the metal corners of the frame had gouged four deep cuts in his palm. *I have graven thee on the palms of my hands*, he thought confusedly, and then lost he rest of the thought as a movement above him made him look up.

The altar had been blown upward to the great chandelier and dangled from it like a trinket.

He could not believe in his own existence. How could it be so? Then he turned and found himself face to face with Saint Benedict's cordial smile. The roly-poly oak saint, who had been a monster to carry, had stayed largely intact and fallen against the wall in such a way that he protected Carlo from debris with his great wooden beer gut, with the branching muscles of his friendly arms.

Carlo stood up. He smoothed out the picture as well as he could and put it back in his wallet. He looked at his watch, which to his astonishment was still ticking. Before leaving town, he would have just time enough to pay a brief visit to the Communist. It wouldn't take more than thirty seconds.

He took a long look at the burning sanctuary. He looked at the place where the altar had been, and where it was now. He said aloud, "Here I am. I'm going to do just fine, you son of a bitch." He picked up his valise, opened the door and left.

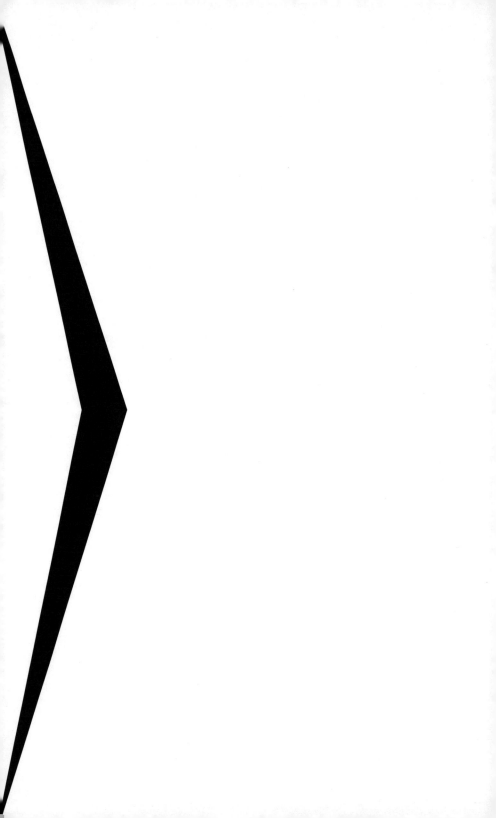

SIMEON PROPHET

Simeon spread the glitter on his woman's fine face with a sparing hand. Too much and she'd look like a hoochie dancer at the carnival. Too little and nobody would know she deserved to shine. He haloed her with a little tiara, glued it on, then licked and slowly placed with his thumb a cloud of tiny gold stars around her head. He stood back and observed the collage. It was not quite right, not worthy of her. He thought about it, then turned to a jumble of greeting cards in a box. He looked through them slowly, one by one. Finally, he found what he wanted, a card with a cat. This he cut out, taking pains not to lose a single hair or claw. He glued the cat in the crook of the woman's elbow. Georgie had never been without her cat. He took a red Magic Marker, and calculated the space, at the bottom of the picture, between two black angels with rhinestone wings. He wrote in small flourishes, Georgie. He looked at it for a long moment. Then he picked up the Magic Marker again and squeezed in two more letters before her name.

Beside Georgie's picture was an assemblage entitled KING of SHAME. It was a likeness of the surgeon who had operated on Georgie and under whose knife she had died. The surgeon had crystal marbles for eyes which gave him the blank gaze of an idiot and an old bleached steer's skull for a head. Upon this, Simeon had twisted the rib bones from a roast into a crazy crown. The surgeon's rapacious purple tongue stuck out with a wedding ring and tiny cross implanted in it, and he had big scythes for arms. Simeon looked at him with hatred.

The air in the studio was steamy with stewing chicken. Simeon filled a plate from the pot on the stove and sat where he could see Georgie's picture as he ate. He knew it was done, but a few feet away was a new painting that wore him out just to look at. So far there was only the outline of a graveyard with a moon looking down, and himself in a long black coat, black boots, and a black hat, laying something on a tombstone. He'd already written the title at the bottom: *I Drop A White Rose On Your Stone*. He thought over the problem of the rose. He wanted that rose to somehow hold up all those gravestones on its tender petals.

By the time Simeon had finished his meal, his head had begun to feel bad. He put his hands to his head. *Spare me, Jesus.* But then he felt ashamed, because it was possible Jesus wanted him to have the migraines. He also noticed that, as always, the more his head hurt, the more clearly he saw everything around him. The delicate joints of the chicken bones curved to each other like coral marvels. He stared at the Yoruba designs on the cobalt blue bowl he held. For the first time, one of them reminded him of a lightning strike, and it seemed to go right through his brain like a burning iron bar. The chicken stew rolled and churned hot around his stomach.

He had just put the bowl down when there was a pounding on the door. At the same time, somebody began shrieking his name. He knew at once who it was. He tried to think if the light in the studio was low enough to fool her into believing he wasn't home.

"Simeon Prophet, I know you're there; you might as well open up first as last." She thumped the door hard. There was the sound of staggering, a fall, and then slow grappling upward with much wrenching at the door knob and ragged breathing.

Simeon's head hurt worse. He shook it, then put both hands to his brow. *I can't put up with her tonight*, he thought. *Nobody could expect it.* "Johanna, go away for now," he said. "I don't feel so good."

Her reply came so loud and so close he knew she had her face pressed right against the window in the door. A jumble of words came out, something like *you phony fucking Christians pretending to be so good but shutting poor folks out like a dog in the cold—*

"Wouldn't they let you in at the shelter?"

"They said I was drunk," she said resentfully. "As if!"

"Can't your husband take you in?" Simeon asked, without much hope.

"Tough love," she said sadly.

Simeon walked over to the side window and looked out. An icy-looking wind was whipping the bare branches. *Pretty damn cold night for tough love,* he thought. But he felt so ill he wasn't ready to give in yet.

"There's nothing to drink here," he said, trying to speak gently, so she would know he wasn't mocking her for her affliction.

There was a long pause. Then she said, in a flat, disheartened voice, "Well, it's cold just the same."

Simeon unlocked the door and big Johanna came in, accompanied by smells so raw and shocking he reeled back. He pretended he'd just been reaching for a chair for her. "Sit here," he said. "I've got some soup."

"I'll heat it," she said eagerly, her eyes traveling over and over the cupboards in the little kitchen. "I'll make coffee, I'll wash dishes."

She would be after the vanilla and the red wine vinegar. "You stay put," he said firmly. He placed the chair for her, and she sat down, arranging the skirts of the horrible men's overcoat she wore. But she shot up again immediately and began to roam the studio. Simeon kept one eye on her as he stood at the stove.

"I can sort beads," she said, fumbling through some shoeboxes of old toys and jewelry. The kids from the grocery co-op had brought those, and he planned to put their faces in his next collage—in a nice way, not as ghosts or devils. "I can cut out decals, I can glue little stones on the borders."

Actually, she could do none of these things, because of her shaking hands. Simeon nodded noncommittally, stirring the soup. As Johanna shambled around the studio, her mighty shoulders stooped over, poking into corners, his gaze sharpened. He thought that because of her size and shaggy dark coat, she looked something like a lady gorilla with a human female's long hair. He began to plan how he could best capture her likeness, maybe with charcoal, and where he could use it. He looked at the new big graveyard painting, barely begun, with himself in the black coat by the tomb, laying a white rose on Georgie's stone. That black night called for a demon or two if anything ever did. Greedily he calculated where to place Johanna, because there was always only one best spot to put a figure in a picture, and it might be no bigger than a dime. He thought she'd fit crouching right on top of the biggest sepulchre, kind of gloating and snarling over the midnight scene, and he would light up all her inflammations with red paint and gilding. He thought, or hoped, that she was too far gone to take offense if he drew her like she was.

The soup boiled over, and Simeon reproached himself. If Georgie had been alive, she would have been leading Johanna to the bathtub right now, laying out the good soap and best towels, and helping her to wash if need be. Thank God he was a man and nobody could expect him to do such a thing.

"*My Georgie*," Johanna read, standing in front of the collage he'd just finished. Her clangy voice, normally all train sounds and metal shards, was almost soft. "This is real nice, Simeon. It looks like her."

Simeon brought the soup to the table. "Come to light, Johanna. Sit down."

She rambled over to the table, and all the time he served her and she ate, his eyes never left her. He studied the curly shamble of her burred hair, her ratty black coat and plum-purple skin with its little snake veins, as though they'd been rich prizes. Her image as he could make it crouched in his brain, stronger than the migraine, matching it beat for beat.

Finally, Johanna was peacefully beached, dozing on the long sofa, which he had covered with a tarpaulin when her back was turned and then with sheets and blankets. He listened to her deep snores. She was dead out.

Simeon lit two candles to work by. Silently, he collected everything he would need for *I Drop A White Rose On Your Stone*, and began to draw. The pain in his head was so bad he could have cried, but he found he could outrun it by working faster and faster to fix Johanna to the picture. Every heaving, hairy part of her vaulted to the top of the sepulchre. He glued pieces of goatskin for her torn boots, scraps of real rat fur and black feathers for the coat, and threads of red yarn radiating all around for the stink. The room was icy cold but he did not feel it. He found himself using techniques he didn't know he had. The sparkling aura of the migraine haloed it all. Every choice he made was as though ordained by God, he couldn't put a step wrong. When he had finally painted and glued and knifed her face glaring out above the demon's gross neck, it shone so thrilling and horrible he almost laughed aloud with pride.

It was hard to tear himself away. He knew the picture was the best he had done, the best he could ever do. But he was dropdown-dead tired, and the room suddenly froze him to the bone.

He went to bed, and in the moment before he fell asleep, he wondered if he would ever be able to conjure up a holy angel half as impressive as the gorgeously terrible Johanna demon.

When Simeon woke up, it was still night. He got out of bed, moving cautiously at first because he didn't know if that migraine fist would come out of the darkness and smite him again, but his head stayed clear. *Thank you, God.* He walked into the studio, trying to be quiet. He was afraid to believe the picture was as good as he remembered it.

Johanna was gone. The blankets and tarpaulin, boxes of beads and toys and bird skeletons were tumbled on the floor. In the past, she had never left until she was driven out, and Simeon began to tremble. He switched the light on, and for a moment kept his head turned away from the picture. But when he finally looked at it, he was still not ready.

Somewhere in the red death train of Johanna's life, she must have had art instruction. No untaught person would have known how to destroy the picture as thoroughly as she did. She had used turpentine, soot, and had even rooted out the acid fixatives that Georgie used to preserve her vegetable dyes. Hardened glue stood thick everywhere on the picture except on the face of the Johanna demon, which squatted on the sepulchre. Here she had taken Simeon's red Magic Marker, circled and slashed the face over and over, and scrawled above it in letters like oak trunks, NOT ME.

Simeon was afraid he would faint with rage and anguish. He shook, and heard himself wailing like some derelict, unfortunate stranger. He thought he had never felt this bad, except when Georgie died. Then he admitted to himself that he had never felt this bad, period, not even when Georgie died. He knew that if Johanna had been in the room he would have cut her down with the hatchet, just chopped her where she stood.

Although he had not yet turned on the heat, his head and body felt as though he was boiling. He walked over to the window, put his face against its icy pane, eyes closed, and wept. When he finally opened his eyes, they were hit by a pearly snow light. The snow was a foot deep. When he moved, he almost tripped over something at his feet. It was a bottle of rubbing alcohol, and it was empty. A hard hateful spitefulness rose in him. His smile was more cruel than that of the best devil he'd ever drawn. *Let her die*, then, he thought.

But he kept looking from the bottle to the snow, the snow to the bottle. He couldn't make his mind leave it alone. He saw her in chalk and charcoal: Johanna dying in the snow. *She's got her damn husband to save her*, he thought. Then he remembered what she'd said, that Lloyd was trying tough love this month. In fact, Johanna had told that to Georgie on her deathbed in December: Lloyd was going to start out the new year with tough love. *Trust Lloyd to choose January*, Georgie had said, smiling sadly.

In the end, it was the thought of Georgie that made Simeon put on his parka and boots. When he stood on the front porch, the cold was shocking. He put his head down and trudged toward the park. He thought there was a good chance she was there. They wouldn't have let her in at the women's shelter, because of the rubbing alcohol.

In the park, Simeon found Johanna in a few minutes. She was snoring peacefully in a snowdrift under a pine, bundled snugly in her big hairy coat, as in the flanks of some huge animal. Simeon was terribly cold, and as he bent down he couldn't help but feel resentful that she looked warm as toast. Suddenly, her eyes snapped open and she glared at him.

"I don't look like in that picture!" she said.

Simeon stared fixedly into the snowy branches of the pine above her head. After a minute he said, "I know it. I know. I was just—" he gestured vaguely.

Greedily scenting a regret she could use, Johanna heaved to her feet and began briskly arranging her mass of coat skirts, mufflers, and fantastic headgear. "I want my breakfast," she said in a hard, commanding voice. Haughtily she swept away, heading for the McDonald's across the street. Her head was high, and she ignored him as a great lady might some disreputable retinue. Simeon followed. She strode out boldly, her big limbs spurning the folds of the black robe-like coat she wore. Her head with all its savage curls was crowned with a bright gold cap plastered with gemmed brooches. She made the whole snowscape jump. It came to Simeon that, from the back, and through his irises dazzled by sunlight, she looked not unlike some high queen.

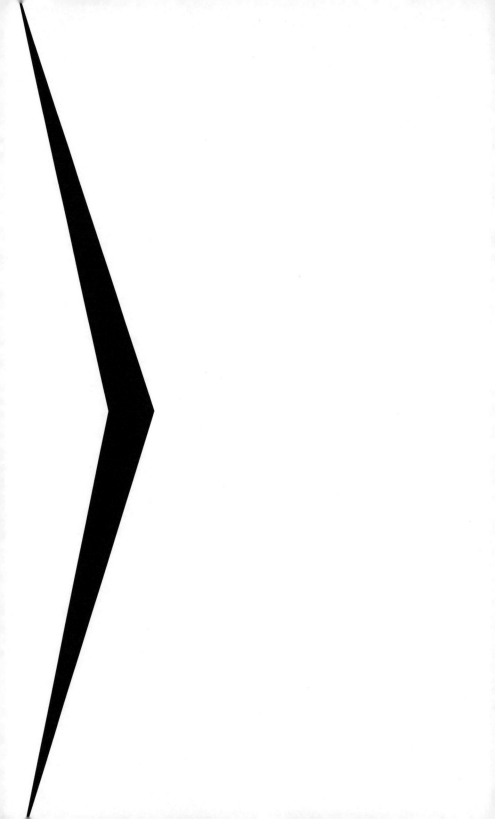

EGYPTIAN

I forget what moron it was who said we should fear no solitude, because there are angels in our midst.

Death changes everything. For example, Sam's and my big bed was no longer the conjugal couch but had become an ancient Egyptian cooling board, which I occupied alone. Night after night, I lay awake as the embalmer, memory, practiced his craft. I lost my brains as surely as though he had drawn them out through my nostril with his little hook. My eyes and heart, lost earlier, waited separately on a platter for use in the afterlife.

I couldn't even write about it. There had never been anything, before, that I couldn't write about. Why, a whole genre existed of widows' memoirs and autobiographical novels in which the dead beloved rose again: to court and marry, to fight, eat vast pasta dinners, swim nude with the dusk on his skin, screw like a bandit, travel, sicken and then die in diamond-cut prose. The widows were not at a loss, they had kept extensive notebooks of their man's fits and starts while he was still breathing. I'd missed my opportunity. I'd lost words while Sam was sick, mislaid the vocabularies of the four languages I speak. The few words I still used during those months were not written down; they were always the same, and they were addressed only to the black beast living and waiting on our roof, his eyes bigger than his stomach: *Are you really going to do this, you evil fuck, you evil motherfucker?*

When Sam had been dead for a year, I tried clumsily to return to life. I still could not write, but I took walks, went to the store instead of having groceries delivered. My friend, Sally, insisted that I had to leave the apartment at least twice a week. I even started dating. Once, I embraced a man on the cooling board, trying to turn it into a bed again. I could not overcome a profound sense of strangeness. What was he doing there, where big Sam had held sway? I became a chaste moon maiden, discreetly shielding yawns, picking bits of mascara off my lashes. My silent apartment was enlivened by a furiously slammed door.

I didn't want him. I didn't want, period.

Now it had been two years. I couldn't write, I didn't date, and my friends had lost patience. Sally, a ferocious mother hen, accused me of wallowing in a rudimentary stage of grief, denial, when by her calculations I should long since have advanced to bargaining with fate. She watched me suspiciously, as though expecting me at any moment to emerge from my seclusion with a Victorian mourning brooch made of Sam's hair clapped to my bosom. Above all, she disapproved of a celibacy, which she considered unseemly. "*Two years?*" she screamed. "It's indecent." In careful language, she pointed out that a passionate attachment to a dead man has no future.

My silence stretched on, became poisonous. Then I said, "You think I need a fuck."

"It wouldn't hurt."

"I'm old."

Sally replied loudly, as though she'd been waiting for this remark: "You are not old. You look ten years younger than your age. Why, the last time you and I went to Schuyler's"—Schuyler had a butcher shop in the next block—"you were wearing that sky blue turtleneck, and I heard Schuyler say real low to Marty, 'I wouldn't mind a piece of that.'"

Well, this was just fucking great. My eighty-year-old butcher had said to his retarded shop assistant that he'd like a piece of me. I wondered which piece. I looked at my hand, small and white; my little left foot, which was beginning to get a bunion.

Sally's practical mind groped for solutions. After researching the topic, she gave me a well-reviewed book that was keyed to those who lack a partner with a beating heart. "Meg, you can't live with this tension," she said as she handed it to me.

The book warmly recommended certain implements, objects, and cruciferous vegetables. However, you could know Mr. Vibrator for ten thousand years and he would never bite your neck. Señor Broccoli will never pass you a cup of tea in bed on a cold morning.

Tension is fine. And I made a secret, revolutionary decision. I would have another human being or nothing.

The new couple in the next apartment had no problems whatsoever experiencing sumptuous crises of desire. I had never seen them but already I knew that they were the busiest damned couple, desire-wise, who ever existed behind a paper wall. I would be at my desk, correcting proofs from the novel I'd finished three years before. At any moment I expected their bed, a four-poster by the sound of it, to engine through the wall spraying plaster and lath and the thrashing manes of its oblivious occupants. I didn't mind the noise as such. It could just as easily have been traffic noise, a siren, a drill, or wrecking ball.

It was fortunate I didn't mind it, because this couple had stamina. I imagined them powered by big lumberman breakfasts, stacks of smoking cakes, bloody steaks, and six or eight fertilized eggs, washed down by Jolt Cola and half a dozen red poppers.

What disturbed me as I tried to work was not the noise, but the human voices, because this couple also talked a lot, and the things they said drew my attention. He had a deep, soft voice, hers was light and almost childish.

He was not exactly brutal, but took a firm, masterful tone. Once, when she objected to something he wanted to do, he said, "I'm not the one you say no to. I'm the one you say yes to."

I'm not the one you say no to. I'm the one you say yes to. That was good; it was tough, meaty, to the point. I hesitated a minute, then reached for my pen. I wrote down what the man said. It was my first note since Sam died. In the next weeks there were many more. Sometimes I would record whole conversations.

The man liked overlord, warrior, and czar images for himself. In moments of highest favor, his girl became his "sweet little queen." It must be good to be king, a long-haired boss tiger prowling around. He said she made him feel as though he had a dozen different animals under his skin. I, scribbling madly to keep up, thought all these animals must be toothed and clawed. He himself was, judging from the sound of his stride, booted and perhaps spurred.

Once he dropped into a chair and said in his soft, coarse voice, "Come here. I'm going to crack you like a whip." The sound of a heavy body assaulting a slight one moved from chair to bed to—the top of the refrigerator? I took extensive notes that afternoon, blue strokes biting into the sheet, wondering all the time what I should do. But her shaken words of love matched his. I dutifully recorded them. I wondered how it could be that these primitive cave words, stark as a rock, could sound so poetic in the woman's small, pink, vaginal voice intertwining with the man's growling moan. I'd thought this was an anthropological experiment I was conducting, recording the life habits of a less evolved tribe. But how could they be less evolved when they were having a better time than I had ever had? I'd never howled for joy. They did.

I didn't know what to think. I didn't know jack. I took notes.

It sometimes seemed to me that the wall between us was the thinnest of membranes through which I could distinguish splendid colors, reds and purples, swelling and waning. At other times the wall seemed like the steel plate door behind which the successful artist guards his perfect works of art.

Once he hit her. She hit him back. Had they reached a degree of intoxication in which anything given by the other's hand seemed good? He cried, and she cried, salt in their kisses. They always said freely what was in their hearts. Sometimes they did crack each other like whips, ending in a sad, plush luxury of sighs. High jinks shattered the light fixtures, she clawed the drapes.

I couldn't quite decide if they'd be together for sixty years, heavy with devotion and seniority, or if next week they'd be discovered by the howling of dogs, the reeling of odors, way past dead.

The night they hit each other, for the first time I read through all the pages of notes I'd been keeping—there were thirty, pretty closely written. Then, without thinking much about it, I reached for a pen and wrote a few paragraphs about a couple named Brett and Shelley. They were not having sex. They were preparing to go to the market. Afterward, they would go to a party. They were new; my new couple. I knew they were mine because I knew what they would do next. And not a thing was going to happen, not a God damned thing, that I did not approve of.

In the next apartment, the man and woman ate a lot of fruit. He said that the skin of her breast was like translucent white plums, which he fed her. She squeezed ripe peaches in her hands, then worked the juice and pulp over his body. He told her to clean him "like a puppy," which she did. One afternoon there were adventures with other fruit.

They really made a lot of noise that afternoon, and to drown it out I laid down my pen and played some Beethoven on my stereo, rather loud. In an instant I heard his furious "Jesus Christ!" then her hesitant tap on the wall.

"I'm sorry," she said in her tiny voice, "could you turn it down?" I turned it down.

When I put the record in its sleeve, I read the album notes and saw that this was the piece, a late one, on which Beethoven had written, "Must it be so?" Beside this someone else had written, in a firm hand, "It must be."

That evening I wrote more about my new couple, Brett and Shelley. At first they did not do anything to anger or startle me. They went to a party. They had good hors d'oeuvres. Then they were dancing, Shelley was watching the pink-bronze sunset over

Brett's shoulder, and suddenly she saw and smelled black smoke. In the next instant, a big gorgeous snake of blue flame crawled through the ceiling, and chunks of charred plaster began falling on the buffet table and in the punch bowl, bobbing beside rose-buds frozen in ice cubes.

I threw the pen down, and stared at my hand. It always frightens me when this happens, and besides, it had been so long since it had.

I got up and left the apartment. It was already dark, but I went to the park where I first met Sam. He had been a formi-dable sight to behold. He was a tall, burly man with shoulders bursting through his old leather jacket, hair half-way down his back, and at his side paced two ferocious-looking hounds. I, who had confidence in nobody, trusted him at once. Within five min-utes, we were sitting side by side on that stone bench.

We became engaged. I introduced him to Sally at lunch. She was aghast. "Meg," she said to me later, "you're a writer. You can't marry a man who holds his meat down with his thumb when he cuts it. I'm afraid to ask what he does for a living."

I looked at her silently. Sally owned many t-shirts that had barbarous but bracing slogans printed on them. Today she was wearing STOP SUCKING, START BITING!

"He works construction," I said.

"He . . . *works construction?*" she repeated, slowly and wonder-ingly, as if noting the gross pre-literate fumblings of an ape man, a man of mud.

"We get on like a house afire," I said in a low voice. "He is it. And that is that."

Who would have guessed, when they saw him, that a gentle heart lived in that mighty house of bone? Or that in the end he would waste to ghost eyes and frog legs? That in the last week, although he was so much taller than I, it was I who supported him everywhere he needed to go?

I stayed in the park very late, remembering all this. I stayed past the time when it was safe, so strong was my sense of his presence. I imagined so clearly his hawkish profile, that gladi-ator's walk of his, and the hounds who were tame to his hand as lambs.

I sat quietly, dreaming. The moon was behind a driving mass of cloud. Time spun itself out, so I don't know which moment it was that I saw a glitter to my right. My mind moved slow-ly to comprehend this. When an object had no source of light, how could it shine? What glittered alone? And indeed the shine, whatever it was, disappeared.

But within a minute, a voice spoke. It said, "Take your clothes off." I looked around wonderingly. Surely this could not be di-rected to me?

A blurry-edged human shape walked slowly toward me from the darkness. "Take your clothes off!" he said, this time in a hard, commanding voice. The blade in his hand had a pretty shine. Did he polish it?

Automatically, I stood up and put my hands to my lapels, then paused. This man had the appearance of the dark real thing, the being and event that we are taught to fear all our lives. But I knew very well that the true dark real thing had happened two years before. This man was an imposter. Normally I'm a timid person, but now a rage began to burn in me, so heady and villainous I could hardly breathe.

For some reason, I remembered the fierce slogans on Sally's t-shirts. Standing there, as the moon began to shift from behind the clouds, I quoted one to him. I said, "YOU MUST BE MISTAKING ME FOR SOMEONE WHO GIVES A FUCK."

He stood silent and still, frozen. Then he raised his blade and started to walk toward me. I glanced wildly around me, scouring the ground for a weapon, and snatched up a jagged broken limb. I waited for him, the limb raised, chanting slogans: "BETTER TO BE TRIED BY TWELVE THAN CARRIED BY SIX." I was not at all afraid. My blood seemed both molten and airy, dying to get at him. "STOP SUCKING, START BITING!"

He reached me and began to raise the blade again, and it was then—"ARE WE HAVING FUN YET, ASSHOLE?"—that I aimed for his head like an axe going down on a chopping block. I put every ounce of power and fury I had into it, and missed him by six inches. I could barely see his stunned face in the darkness. He almost looked as though he were commiserating with me. I raised the tree limb, tried again and this time did manage to get a piece of his shoulder. He came up with an odd, almost girlish little scream, like a wounded rabbit.

Now I knew I could do it; I kept flailing away at him, sometimes hitting, more often missing, but trying my best. He seemed paralyzed with astonishment. His knife hand sagged. There was the solid dead sound of the wood hitting his coat. I'm convinced I would have stood there and belabored his sorry body with the hardwood until one of us caved in like an orange crate, except that after perhaps half a minute the limb was lifted out of my hands from behind. It was taken from my clenched fists lightly, easily, as though by a giant or an angel. I almost fainted with shock. I flinched away, threw my arms up to protect myself, and saw a huge figure standing over me. In the dark I made out the lines of a massive shape, mighty-shouldered, clothed in a great-coat. Long, rich hair flowed over these shoulders. *Sam's ghost?* I thought hysterically. Then the deep voice of my neighbor spoke. Apparently he'd been out for his evening stroll. "What do you plan to do, nudge him to death?" he said. "The dumb fuck isn't worth it. Go home."

I went home, shaking. Behind me I heard screams, none of them apparently my neighbor's. I did not turn to look.

That night, Brett died in the fire. Shelley did everything she was supposed to do—*Stop, drop, and roll*—but she could save only herself, not him. Hysterically, she threw the punch bowl with its icy roses in the direction of the flames, but that made it worse. She was scooped up by a monster in strange fetish regalia who turned out to be a fireman; she mightily fought him with head-butts and kicks of both arms and both legs, trying to stay where Brett was, but the fireman seemed to be a man without mercy. A woman who dies in a fire has very little pain at the end because the nerve endings are destroyed; yet the fireman insisted on saving Shelley and carried her out into the night in her smouldering chiffons.

At this point I laid my pen down. I remembered vowing to myself that nothing would happen to Shelley and Brett that I did not approve. Yet here they were, one dead against my will, one alive against my will, their every pore, tooth, and hair lit up in the conflagration of their story. *Story.* "God damn," I said aloud.

"I want you to try it. Please."

They were at it again, next door.

"No."

"Baby, please," he said. " I've always loved cosmetics made from minerals, like the Egyptians used. Cleopatra was too much. Do it for me."

She said no. He said, "Did you know kohl is black powder made from lead ore? And they used to paint their lips with red ochre. I found a shop, I've got it here. Look what I got for you. Please."

She made some indistinct sounds, tears and words. I heard, "I'm not a doll," in a sob. I was trying to revise my new manuscript, and was annoyed.

He didn't hit her. He talked to her sweeter than I've ever heard a woman talked to, ever been talked to, in my life. And she cried harder than I've ever heard a woman cry. She cried so hard my hand hovered above 911. But what could I tell them? That he was committing abuse by cosmetics? And whom would they send? Firemen didn't seem right.

At last she said yes. He said, "Come over by the mirror. Start with the eyes. I love that elongation at the end of the eye. It should be shaped like a leaf. Smudge it a little. Then the mouth, outline it in red, it should look heavy and soft. I could go crazy for a woman with a mouth like that. A little gold on the lids. Nobody dares touch your gold but me. They want it, but they can't touch. The eyebrows should be heavy, black and straight—"

I heard a chair sway and creak. He was leaning back as he watched. He said, "Throw me one of those pears while you're at it." I heard the round smack of the pear hitting his palm. I pictured him, big-jointed, carnal-smelling, that rich hair down his back, his long fingers dripping with pears.

Oh, man, I thought. *Oh man alive.*

I wanted to see him. If possible to meet him. I listened to their preparations for departure, matched my step to theirs, burst out of my street door at the same instant they left theirs.

Anybody would have noticed her exceptional fairness and her beauty. She was ornately and seductively dressed, her bodice top full of flesh bloom as a rose is of petals. You would see also that she was a very large woman, a noble female vista. Her mane of chestnut hair fell over the mighty back and shoulders of an Amazon queen.

A dark man walked at her side. He was the most handsome man I had ever seen, in miniature. His head came to her heart. He made me think of a graceful Sherpa god, proudly flushed from scaling her thrilling gradients. I noticed that the woman's bloom was natural, accented by sweat on her brow and upper lip. He, however, had been exquisitely made up, the eyes lengthened with kohl, the red mouth heavy and soft.

But above all you would notice the tender accommodation each made to the other, so that although she was so large, and he so small, their bodies and postures dovetailed perfectly, they walked like twins.

Momentarily he turned his head when we passed. "Beautiful day, isn't it?" he said.

I nodded, and as he smiled, his lids gleamed gold.

GABRIEL DESPERADO

The big garlic-breathing snake of penitents whips its coils up and down the church aisles. Whew, this parish has to be God's funkiest ever. I'm one of the snake's links, and like everyone else, I back with tiny steps toward the confessional. Our faces must always be turned to the altar and the cross—a sort of phototropism, although anything less like sunflowers than some of these faces you would never see. Behind me is the mountain of spices that is Mom. Now she's talking. "Tell him everything, Gabriel!" she hisses to me, her baby man. "Everything, everything!"

For my whole life, seventeen years, she's seen trouble coming. She saw it like a dead lamb on her doorstep, its throat slit and a note around its neck: *your lamb's next.* She saw it when I was her twig-like infant son, a birthmark between my brows like a tiny hoof of Diablo. She smelled it in the creases of my First Communion suit. With passion, unceasingly, she probed my still waters for signs of snake. For sixteen years, I tried to reassure her, studying hard, star pupil, nose clean. But somewhere in there—fourteen, fifteen, sixteen—I began to sense the lusciousness of her torment. I alone, of her twelve children, held her full gaze. She had taken my projected doom deep into her big cabbage-rose heart. My fate cankered and she suffered, but in what voluptuous company: all the major saints.

"Don't you understand, Gabriel?" she would say softly, when I'd done something wrong—and how tiny they were, my wrongdoings: like grains of sand. "Because of our name" she meant Desperado "—we have to be twice as good as anyone else."

Why not just change the fucking name? I thought. But I didn't say it.

She tried her best to keep me on track. Every morning she walked me to school, holding my hand, and every afternoon she was waiting at the gate. I didn't mind being guarded. Precious things are guarded. Elvis Presley's mother walked him to school until he was seventeen. Mom scanned the rooftops for snipers, kept her body between mine and drug dealers. Everybody knew that Annunziata Desperado would take a bullet for her son. This was a neighborhood where, if you weren't quick, you were dead. Actually, she got me out fairly early. Her nursing jobs did it. She carried us all out on her back.

You have to realize that my mother was a nationally recognized, certified heroine. She'd once saved a dozen babies from a burning hospital. Dead babies? Not on *her* watch. There was a famous photograph of her that ran in every newspaper in the country. She was wearing a special coat with ten big pockets, which they have to move babies in emergencies. Newborns flared up from her shoulders like wings, bulged at her hips like holsters, formed immense breastlike mounds in front, with their bobbing bald heads. Two kicked at her heels, two at her toes, and she carried one baby in her right arm. The left arm she had to use to push aside burning timbers, so they never did figure out how she got the twelfth baby out.

I think myself that she balanced it on her head. She was pictured just after emerging from a wall of flame, a calm, radiant smile on her face. Kneeling sobbing at her feet and kissing her white nurse's shoes was Sandro the Cobra, a local gangster so fearsome we'd been forbidden even to say his name. He'd once bitten off an enemy's nose and eaten it. But his little granddaughter was the miraculous twelfth baby, the one no one else could have saved, and so he said to my mother, "Anything, Doña. Anything you ask. Whatever you wish. My whole life long."

As I said, my mother made serious attempts, right through, to preserve me. But she had grave doubts.

Her suspicions came to a head around the time I turned seventeen. One afternoon, my friend Billy was visiting, and in the upstairs hall he said to me, "I missed you, man. Does your mother know what we do?" Billy meant: does she know we smoke pot? But sitting in the tub, my mother—an orchidaceous brown atoll in which my father has planted his flag at least five thousand times—took it differently. She screamed. I'm surprised she didn't electrocute herself, dropping the hair dryer, fireballs rolling off her kinks, zapping her butt right up to glory. She came charging out like one of those big-ass fertility goddesses with a bath towel thrown around her—a sight I expect to see on my deathbed— and she did her absolute best to beat me like a dog while keeping the bath towel secured. I stopped her the only way I knew how, yanking it off. She never forgave me; I never forgave her.

Things changed. Before that bath, all my life it had been, "I love you, my pure and perfect Gabriel, and your little toes too." But after the bath, I'd stopped being Mama's imperiled pearl and was now a heaving mass of smut and junk, phosphorescent with moral decay.

I could've sworn I was straight, but she knew better. Whoops, *don we now our gay apparel*. In fact, she thought I did everything with everyone, like Freddie Mercury. We saw doctors, psychiatrists, saints. My mother, like all the other good women in this neighborhood, is valued for all the things which she, with a proud queenliness, refuses to do. I gained an instant, fiery notoriety for the things she thought I did do. A certain kind of mother thinks her teenage son spends his life walking up to drug dealers and saying, "I'll do anything for a fifty dollar rock." My mother also believed I spent every night running down nameless warmbloods on the street.

Under the circumstances, it seemed tactless to mention my virginity.

Now backing slowly, I find myself beside a nativity painting. Mary has the faintly hairy upper lip, the vast dark eyes of the

Middle East, which makes sense. She doesn't have one of those submission-bleached sheep faces you find in Flemish Madonnas. Actually, she looks a lot like my mother, about twenty years back on the road.

It was after the bath I said to myself, *All right, Mama, let's go.* I cut the sleeves off my grandmother's fur coat and wore it over a fishnet body stocking. I began leaving little dabs of white powder in my pockets. It was baking powder, although she couldn't be sure. I would see her licking it off a forefinger, as she'd seen on TV. Her brow, broad and mild like a good child's, was creased in doubt. "It tastes like baking powder," she was thinking. "On the other hand, maybe cocaine—or horse, snow, junk, whatever they call it—does taste like baking powder." She is nothing if not thorough, my mama. Even with her heart splitting in sections like an orange, she would pursue every avenue of speculation as far as her motherly walls would allow—short, that is, of discussing it with someone who would actually know.

Sometimes I would put a little blood on my clothes, my boxer shorts—not much blood, but blood where it ought not to be. I could just see her, with trembling lips, turning this over in her mind. My mama's mind is like God's mills: it grinds slowly, but it grinds exceedingly small. I could tell she was thinking hard, trying to decide which explanation for the blood was worse: for it to be a stranger's blood, making Gabriel a thug; for it to be Gabriel's blood, the result of unspeakable practices; or for Gabriel to have been in some place so terrifying that blood was just in the air. She would almost fall into a diabetic coma at such a sweet plenitude of disaster. What a field of honey.

Still, to this day she continues to have great faith in the curing ceremony of the confessional, and so it's been Confession for Gabriel every Saturday afternoon. My mama believes the priest can save her possessed boy, charm my dark. She thinks that during one of these sessions, sooner or later, the priest will get a really good headlock on me spiritually, and the demons will pour forth from ears, nose-holes, every orifice (including the most defiled), screaming for mercy. I will stop inhaling, exhaling, snorting. I will stop grieving Jesus with my lust.

The truth is that I enjoy the confessions. I spend a lot of time beforehand perfecting my presentation. I've always spent hours every day reading and studying, and the weekly confession report seems very natural. I dig deep and scheme and embellish. Somehow the situation reminds me of a quote I heard in French class: "One must go into himself armed to the teeth." That's Paul Valéry. Also, my big Ancient Roman History book has been a surprising help. I've laid claim to some of Caligula's more spectacular stunts, slightly adapted, of course. The priests are too uneducated to recognize the source.

I like a three-dimensional presentation with audio, visual, and aroma coordinates. I study my pictures of John Brown and Lizzie Borden, look into their laser eyes. They both look like crackheads if I ever saw one. I select clothes with the care a surgeon might lavish on transplant organs. Mom always said I was too thin-skinned. Look at me now, my rhinoceros hide thick with fur, leather, and rubber. My family doesn't know it, but they all contribute: on Confession days I drizzle my pulse points with model airplane glue, and Black Orchid scent, and Johnny Walker Red.

Sometimes I smell so high that Mom and I have a five-foot clearance around us in the Confession line. However, she immediately turns this into an enchanted protectorate, a noble vantage from which we survey the less fortunate. Her strong, calm gaze indicates her belief that my worst deeds and worst smells are intrinsically better—more valuable, lovable, and interesting—than the best deeds and best smells of other people's children. Her proud carriage says: it's true that Gabriel suffers, temporarily, from an affliction which impels him to break every single Commandment, every single day. However, when this derangement ends, as it will, he will resume his true place as the prince of everything.

Oh—I forgot to mention what I do about physical evidence, like rips and burns. Sometimes I fake it, sometimes not. This morning I paid Billy's brother Tashawn to bash me on the face with a block of wood, for the sake of a magnificent bruise. You must suffer for art.

When I came into our house afterward, Mama said, "Where did you get that?" Naturally she had noticed the bruise. It was the size of a child's baseball glove. I had commissioned a bruise that would be noticed. With proud modesty, I slowly turned my face away so that only the great, smeared, blunt-force trauma of the blow showed.

"Mama," I said with deadly gentleness, "in the kind of life I lead, there will be some wear and tear."

She didn't say anything for a minute. Then she said just one word, "Tashawn," so quietly I hardly heard her. She didn't cry, shout, or hit me on my good cheek. Expressionlessly, she changed the direction of her eyes, and I couldn't help turning my head to see what she was looking at. It was one of those ghastly paintings of the Pietà that she loves so much. There are five in our house. This one shows a small, gnarled, humpbacked Mary hauling about and attempting to lift a lubberly Christ. He must weigh at least two hundred and fifty pounds.

She said only, "Get ready for Confession. We'll leave in ten minutes."

In the last weeks, my Confessions have become magnificent, soaring from strength to strength. Maybe it's because I spend so much time hanging out with Tashawn, who is full of ideas. I push this dark, shimmering life straight through the iron flowers of the grill. I'm glad if the priest is Father Karl, who has eyes like a drug dog. He's a club-fisted, muscle-bound Pole who is visibly sickened, appalled, disgusted, and enraged by my life. He's told me that he'd cheerfully beat me to death just to get me back on track. You can get your teeth into a priest like that.

On the other hand, I'm sorry if it's Father Len. He studies the macerated design of my life with such quiet hopelessness. It lies there, vibrating, and he pokes it sadly, like a voodoo sorcerer hired to harvest potent truths from chicken guts. He feels so bad I'm afraid he'll start to cry. I'll be enjoying myself, saying to him in a creepy voice, *"We do it quietly. We do it at night. We do it so that nobody can watch——"* and his lip trembles so much I'm worried for him. I'm tempted to say something positive, just to cheer him up a little. You know, like, "Yoo-hoo, Father Len, guess what? I'm not as big a crackhead as I used to be, and I have a crush on Santina Emory. That's some hot Catholic girlmeat, yumm! And you know what a good girl she is, just as good as she can be. I wouldn't rule out a big white wedding down the road—no, I wouldn't rule it out at all."

I once heard on the radio, during some speech, "You are where your deep driving desire is." So many people are absolutely certain they know where my desire is. I myself have no idea.

Of course all charades end. Mine must. I noticed long ago that law-abiding people are fascinated by reformed renegades, human brands snatched from the burning. They like them much better than those who've been good all along. For example, after Tashawn put a brick through his aunt's face, it's amazing how his family rallied behind him. Today, a year later, he's leaping the highest in a dance troupe of delinquents our church is sponsoring. This is only one example. There are dozens I could give. My reformation, properly handled, could yield many satisfactions, not excluding fat scholarships.

I'm notorious in the neighborhood, my mother's cross. Yesterday at the market we saw the neighborhood gangster Sandro the Cobra choosing produce, leaving fierce thumb holes in the cantaloupes. He looked at me, at my face, particularly at my eyes with my pupils like soft black dahlias—the effect of belladonna drops, not drugs, although he had no way of knowing—and he looked at my mother with pain and compassion.

"Are you satisfied?" she said to me later, bitterly. "Sandro the Cobra is sorry for me."

So I can't give it up yet. I enjoy the cozy hours in my room, sculpting the basic shape of the Confession, placing its adornments. In the booth, I like the spoor of shock bolting through the priest's black clothes, his dropped jaw. After all, my story to him is that not only do I ingest every evil substance known to historical man, but that I'm a monster of potent carnality, my seductiveness cannot be withstood by man, woman, or beast of the field. Now, I could tell this to any kid in the street, and he'd take one look at me and laugh his ass off. But the priests believe it. Not only do they accept that I am irresistible, irresistible; they see it as their absolute duty to present this to me as a terrible misfortune.

Lately, Tashawn has been asking me to go along with him on his night circuits; just to stand at his side and learn. He says that imagination can only take me so far, that some genuine local color would jolt my Confessions over the top into greatness. It would knock the priest right off his chair. I said I would think it over, and I have. I will tell him yes after Confession today. He'll be waiting at the church door. He said there's an interesting older man he wants me to meet. I look forward to seeing Tashawn, his "eyes of steel in a choirboy's face," as my French literature book says about Rimbaud.

"Next!" It's Father Karl's voice, thank God.

I stalk into the confessional, armed to the teeth. My hair is ratted up from my head a full ten inches high. I'm fishnet and snakeskin from the waist up, spandex from the waist down. I got a little angel dust from Tashawn and patted it on my cheeks like aftershave. Usually, when my mother and I get ready for church there's an enjoyable five minutes listening to her scream about my outfit before we leave the house. But today she was having a very intense conversation on the phone, and I thought I heard her call the person Sandro—holy shit, is she going to call in that favor he promised, maybe have his goons kidnap me and deprogram me from my one-person sin-and-damnation cult? And in the car I asked and asked. But she said nothing.

Father Karl's nostrils jump as he picks up the peppermint smell of the angel dust. I nail him dead in the eye with my raging Lizzie Borden glare. He glares straight back, and I can tell he's itching to bash through the grille and strangle me like a rat.

Although I'm armed, I haven't decided what will happen in the next few minutes. I'm attracted to the idea of winging Father Karl, but he'd probably take the opportunity to rip my nose off. Today, I'll just show a discreet flash of steel: less mess, less fuss. I'll still be able to meet Tashawn. And my mother is here. Behind me I sense the warm rose shadows of her dress, not to mention the flaring lily horn of her ear.

In a panting whisper I speak about execrations, violations, assassinations, and all the while I'm half-killed by Father Karl's breath. It reeks of the nasty kielbasa he favors, the kind where nothing in the pig is left out. This happens so much that Tashawn and I have talked about it. "What kind of priest eats hog guts right before he's going to hear forty or fifty Confessions?" Tashawn asked furiously. "The sadistic son of a bitch does it on purpose. A man like that ought to be shot down like a dog." Tashawn's hard amber eyes sparkled with incomparable intensity.

Every moment, even in the confessional, I wonder what it would be like to do the things the ferocious ones do. To be like Tashawn. Then at last I could look into my mother's face, just look at her and say, *Congratulations. I am as wicked as you believe.*

Now Father Karl is reaching the climax of his fulminations in a geyser of spittle, and I'm half-fainting from his breath. I'm aware of the gun in my pocket, a sweet little steel prize tempting my hand. In fact, I'm so aware of it that when all of a sudden I hear screeching tires and those sharp, loud cracks outside by the church door and a kid screaming as though his guts have been shot out, those sounds we all know, I stupidly open my pocket and stare at the gun in shock, just to make sure it didn't jump into my hand and make me a murderer. Now there are crowd sounds outside, shouts of panic, somebody wailing "Tashawn's dead!" and car doors slamming and then a car speeding away, and more shouting and crying. I stumble out of the booth. I turn to my mother, as I always have, and she puts her warm, calm arms around me. She doesn't look frightened at all. Where have I seen that radiant smile before?

"I would do anything for you, Gabriel," she says softly. "Anything. *Para ti.*"

Y TODOS DEBEMOS MORIR:
AND WE MUST ALL DIE

The Spanish boy had been missing for two weeks. Campus police had stopped interviewing other students, search parties had been called off, even his parents had gone back home to Andalusia. It was, after all, dead in the middle of the most bitterly cold winter in anybody's memory. No corpse had been found, and it was theoretically possible that one of these days he'd crop up, maybe climb off the Greyhound from Las Vegas, clutching his winnings, smoking a cigar, and with a wild Hawaiian shirt under his puffy parka. But nobody was counting on it.

His roommate, Chad, had gone back to drinking himself blind at the Kollege Klub, telling people in a beery whisper that it was kind of a relief not to have to listen to Javier's crappy opera records anymore. What kind of freak owned a turntable, anyway? Also Javier had started praying aloud in the middle of the night, which creeped out the girls Chad brought back to their dorm room. Word was that Javier's rich family had sent him to America to get rid of him, because he was weird and was an embarrassment to them. So although Chad hoped the strange little guy hadn't suffered, whatever had happened to him, "It's an ill wind, you know what I mean?"

Although Javier was not popular among the other students, he did have one friend, a girl named Jane Huntley. Jane could understand what he said in spite of his heavy accent. They would walk all over campus excitedly talking about opera.

Jane was tall and athletic in build, while Javier was short and slight. As they strode along, there were some students who made fun of them.

"Have you climbed that mountain yet, Javier?" Ben Stewart shouted. His friends Josh and Terry looked on, grinning. Ben was a very popular boy, a football player.

Javier answered with a bewildered smile. He didn't understand what Ben meant. He thought he was being pleasant for once. Jane glared, and stored names. Josh Greer, she thought. *Terry Thornton. Ben Fucking Stewart.*

Jane had a turntable, and so Javier would bring over his old classical records and they would listen to them together. The first time, he stood on her doorstep with his records in his arms, and looked at the Catholic church across the street. It was a beautiful old church, known for its architecture and rose window.

"What a blessing for you, to live so close to it," he told Jane seriously. He hesitated, searching for the phrase he wanted. "In its arms."

Jane, who was an atheist, listened to this respectfully but said nothing. She was thinking to herself that she had never seen a white person with eyes and hair so black. His hair fell over his thin shoulders in vigorous curls. His gaze was unusually direct and clear, like a child's. This pure, intent look of his was one of the things she liked about him, but when she knew him better, it made her afraid for him.

Javier especially liked the opera *Turandot*. He explained to Jane that it was about a prince in disguise, Calaf, who undertakes impossible tasks to win the proudly virginal and beautiful Princess Turandot. He played Calaf's song "Nessun Dorma" and translated it from the Italian in a soft, dreamy voice:

> *In your chaste bower, watch the stars trembling with hope and love…my love lies hidden within me, no one shall discover my name! oh no, I will reveal it only on your lips when daylight shines forth!…and at dawn I shall win! I shall win! I shall win!*

He never touched Jane, but she knew he had a passionate, romantic temperament by his expression during the intense parts of the opera. "*Y todos debemos morir,* and we must all die," Javier translated for himself and for her in a muted voice, and he shook his head, pitying the fate of the princess's tragic suitors.

Finally he confided to Jane his love, which he feared was hopeless, for his physics teacher's young wife, Suzanne. He considered the professor a cold kettle of fish. Javier thought that nobody should blame beautiful Suzanne for having affairs, and in fact only he knew about them, because he followed her continually. It was such a very cold winter that everybody was dressed in gorilla-thick hooded stormcoats. It was hard to tell who came here, who went there. But he, Javier, could recognize Suzanne even when he saw no more than her pink ear, or the heel of her boot as she ran around a corner at midnight. Nobody but he could understand the adventurousness and stunning boldness of his love; nobody but he had seen her skate, laughing, so close to the cataract with her newest fool. She was like Princess Turandot in the opera, he said: she asked everything, she took everything, but to the right man, she would also give everything. Someday she would notice him, Javier said, and she would realize his steely mettle. It was for that reason that he followed her everywhere, no matter what the weather, and watched and waited for her. It was cold work, but it was all for her. He even armed himself to protect her in case the fools in question found out about each other. He held up a knife with an intricately carved handle and a long, leaf-thin blade.

"My *poignard,*" he said. "It has been in my family for generations."

Jane hesitated. Finally she said, "Our country is not Turandot's country, Javier. Here, people would say you were stalking Suzanne."

"But that is not what I am doing at all. I am saving her," he said. "I would die to protect her. A heart like hers, so sensitive, would understand this."

Jane kept his secret. She saw him grow thinner and thinner, the flesh falling from his bones. She knew that he stayed out half the night, rarely slept, that he had almost stopped going to classes, that he went out in the monstrous cold in his thin black jacket instead of the expensive parka his parents bought for him. When Jane urged him to wear the parka, he corrected her, but tried to do so in a manner that would not make her feel foolish. He was always gentle.

"I thank you for your concern. You are a friend to me. But the day will come when Suzanne sees me. I must be dressed for it. Prince Calaf wore black in the opera. He would never wear a parka."

He would turn up at Jane's place in the hour before dawn, half dead with cold and exhaustion, but exalted, full of stories of his hunt that night for elusive Suzanne. She liked to run through the winter wilderness with her lovers no matter what the hour or weather, as duller folk lay stultified like oxen in their beds. She would dart before him, a flaming rose of a princess, almost as though she knew he was there and was leading him on a spirited chase over the icy hills and through the trees with some big lummox lover floundering pitifully in her footsteps.

Jane fed him when she could, gave him boiling homemade soups in which she'd submerged chunks of beef for strength, many garlic cloves and onions, heavily salted and peppered. He ate sloppily, looking up from the bowl, his gaze shining and visionary, red patches flaring on his blade-thin cheekbones.

"I think she might have seen me tonight," he would say happily. "I hid, but the tree was really too small to conceal me. Now she is going with Ben Stewart. She was beating that big idiot with a branch and laughing. I laughed too, to myself. It was almost as though we were laughing together. What a woman!"

A week later, in the hour before dawn, Jane was watching for him as usual. The weather had been indescribably bad. There was a sleet storm so heavy she couldn't believe that even Javier, warmed by his obsession, had gone out in it. Suddenly she noticed a small dark form collapsed on the steps of the church across the street. It looked like a dead animal. She thought she recognized Javier's jacket. Crying out she ran through the storm in her pajamas and up the church steps. It was Javier. He couldn't stand. She carried him back across the street, fumbled at her door, and stumbled with him into her warm living room.

In the lamplight, she saw he had a terrible bruise on his face. He made no response to her questions. He seemed too shocked, or stunned, to speak. She wrapped him in blankets, made him sit beside the register and turned the heat up in the room. She boiled coffee for him and poured brandy in it. She tried to say calm, normal things. It was several minutes before he was able to speak.

"I thought if only I could get inside the church," he said. "Right inside the sanctuary." He was shaking and shaking. "This Ben Stewart," he said. "This Ben." She waited, and after a minute he continued. "I never liked the look of him. I fear she is not safe with him. I've tried to keep close, to watch over her, and tonight I walked her home."

"You walked with her?" Jane asked in astonishment.

"Well, half a block back. I kept behind parked cars. She said goodnight to him at her door, and the door closed, and as soon as she was gone, that violent animal Ben ran back down the street straight toward me and hit me with all his strength. He shoved me down and kicked my body. I thought I was being killed. Then he walked away laughing. Oh, she is in terrible peril, and I don't know how to keep her safe." He put the mug down and began wringing his hands.

"Are you injured?" she cried out. "Did he break your ribs? Show me!" In a panic she began opening his shirt.

He gently put her hands away. "It doesn't matter," he said. "I will not flatter that fool by acting as though his beastliness is important."

"Javier," she said, "you have to stop. This has gone too far. Aren't you afraid of what could happen, something even worse?"

He stood suddenly, the blankets falling to the floor, and his dark eyes burned at her as he passionately framed the swollen bruise of his face with both hands. "What do you think this is, a black dahlia? Of course I am afraid. But who but me will protect her against that brute beast? She needs me more than ever."

And nothing Jane said could dissuade him.

Two nights later, he didn't appear. He was absent the next day, and the next. The police search began, and their spokesman said gravely that the search was compromised because the ground was scoured by continual storms. They had found his warm parka in his room. Jane looked for him, privately, frantically, everywhere she could think of.

Late one night, she was returning home after one of her searches. She hardly knew which night. They flowed into each other. The falling snow was heavy and soft. She didn't know if the ice on her face was from the sky or from her eyes. She noticed a man walking ahead of her, and saw from his fashionable military coat with its epaulets, and his brush-cut blond hair, that it was Ben Stewart. She tightened her hood until it covered every part of her face except her eyes.

Jane walked faster until she was right behind him. She grabbed his shoulders and wrenched him around to face her. He skidded on the icy sidewalk and fell sprawling on the cement. He was momentarily stunned. He made a sound, a startled groan. She began to kick him, without a word, without hurry. The kicks seemed to come from outside herself, from some efficient engine in her boot. Finally she felt she had done enough and was about to leave, when she remembered the terrible bruise on Javier's face. She lifted Stewart's head by its hair and slammed him three times in the face with her fist. She put her mouth to his ear and whispered two words: *"For Javier."* Then she walked away.

The next morning she passed Ben Stewart as she walked to class. He turned his battered face away and said nothing.

The fifteenth night, she sat up and played Javier's opera records for hours, one after the other. The blizzard had stopped and through the window, she saw a night sky of crystalline clarity, swept with stars. She played Javier's recording of *Turandot* and thought, *Y todos debemos morir.* She was putting the record back in its sleeve when she suddenly remembered something she'd told Javier: only a few words, months before, and he hadn't even seemed to be listening. *But they already looked there,* she thought.

She dressed in her heavy hooded peacoat, muffler, and gloves. Storms were over, but this was the coldest night yet. Jane started out at 1 a.m. For an hour, she walked over ice and snow. Not a person, and only a few cars, passed her as she walked. Finally, she reached North Point Woods. The police had already searched here, tormented by blizzards. She stumbled through the woods, the snow packed higher than her boots, to its furthest corner. There was a tiny grove there, although you would not know it if you saw the place now, submerged in snow banks and collapsed evergreen branches. Two years before, as a shy new student, Jane would come here alone and read poetry. "My place," she said to herself. It was a perfect place to hide. She had told Javier about it once, in passing, just as an illustration to prove how far she'd come in gaining confidence. She no longer hid from people. She sat and read in the open, on the library lawn, like everybody else. And so would he, someday.

The evergreen boughs had been shattered by heavy snow, were intertwined and hard to move. Patiently, Jane eased them free, one by one. When she had put the last one aside, crouching, she looked up, and found herself face to face with Javier.

He was sitting on the ground, a silver boy all covered with ice from his black curly hair to the shabby tennis shoes, which he wore no matter what the weather. His black eyes, framed in glittering ice lashes, looked into her own. She had never seen him look so beautiful. There was a white paper stuck to his chest over his heart, she didn't understand how it stayed in place, then saw the ornate handle protruding. Kneeling close to him, she gently worked the paper loose until it fell away from the blade. She studied it in radiant moonlight, which poured into the little grove.

"I know your name, you little creep," the letter began, in a curly, feminine hand. "You pathetic fool, stalking me all the time…I'll tell the police…I'll tell my husband and he'll get you expelled…go back to fucking Spain…me and Ben will make you wish you were dead." Black blotches concealed other words.

He couldn't live in the same world as that letter. Slowly, Jane folded the stiff paper and put it in her pocket. It was nobody's business why he had done it. They hadn't earned the right to know.

She put her arms around Javier, and rested her head against his. She stayed with him for a long time, although she felt herself growing numb. She realized finally that she would have to get up and leave him, or die with him.

She kissed him once. She began to stand up, and for the first time noticed that he had something clutched in his left hand. It was a rosary. As she stared at it, an idea occurred to her. She was tall and strong, and Javier was small. She thought that she might be able to carry him back. He had always loved the Catholic church in her neighborhood. She thought that she might be able to get him inside somehow, and lay him on the altar. He would be found soon, but for a few hours he'd lie in state. She knew Prince Calaf deserved to be there, even if no one else did. *A friend is someone who knows your real name.*

She braced one hand on Javier's shoulder, and with the other wrenched the knife out of his breast. She threw it aside without looking at it. Then she tightened both arms around him, strained upward until she could feel warm blood flowing again in her own heart, and lifted him out of the ice.

IN THE MIDNIGHT HOUR

"I've got a splitting headache," Jeremy said.

Maria stopped brushing King Bolo's fur. She didn't say so, of course, but she wondered why Jeremy never just had a headache like other people. It was always a *splitting* headache. "Did you take pills for it?"

"No," he said, his hands at his temples. "It's not a real solution to dope yourself up." He permitted himself a small glance at her drink, her cigarette burning on the end table, then threw himself full-length on the sofa, where she always read at night. He shielded his eyes to show that the lamp was driving red-hot anvils into his brain. His lips were clamped together, expressing pain and fortitude. Jeremy had a small, exquisite mouth that looked as though it were always on the verge of tasting, or saying, or doing, something unspeakably delicious. Maria considered it dispassionately. Sometimes she thought she had married him because of that mouth. And then, as things had turned out—

Well. She turned out the lamp. She took her drink and cigarette and went to the kitchen. She turned around at the door and said hesitantly, "About supper—"

"Oh, Christ, Maria!" His narrow shoulders writhed into the sofa cushion, expressing impatience, agony, his head splitting.

She turned the heat off in the oven, fumbling a little because of her hand. She put the tray of appetizers back into the refrigerator, the thawing cheesecake into the freezer. It was odd how many suppers they ended up not eating. Of course, Jeremy had always been difficult about food. At times, over the dinner table, she could see so clearly the kind of petulant, finicky little kid he'd been, driving his mother crazy, his reed neck turning *No* to greens and fresh farm eggs, his pouty mouth turning down at the corners and refusing passage to steaks gleaming with juice, to glasses of home-squeezed orange juice. Jeremy's mother, who was a poet, visited them often. Usually, she and Jeremy spent the time fighting about his refusal to accompany her to the Episcopalian Church. "If God was good enough for T.S. Eliot, he's good enough for you," she told him vigorously.

If Jeremy happened to be gone, Mrs. Fulton would talk to Maria, although in a carefully pitched and phrased voice. Because Maria was from Hawaii and had been a painter, and did not teach literature or write, Mrs. Fulton always assumed that she did not quite understand English. She treated Maria just a bit as though she were a nut-brown maiden Jeremy had brought home by catamaran from a distant sea island, or even lassoed and pulled down from a tree, an unbrassiered innocent with Brillo-like kinks of hair erupting from her head, berries and guavas squashing between her bare toes. Mrs. Fulton felt it safest to keep their conversations simple.

Just once, she confided in Maria, and of course it was about Jeremy and food. Mrs. Fulton said that she had always particularly regretted his hatred for orange juice. It would have turned his insides healthy, she thought, as though each corpuscle was armed with tiny gleaming-leaved citrus trees bobbled with fruit. She told Maria more. She had always been terrified by Jeremy's skinniness as a child. She would coax him with terrible patience and gentleness to eat, eat, eat, but in reality she wanted to seize him by the birdy shoulders, whack her forehead against his forehead, drill him in the eye with her eye and snap, *Okay, young man, fun time's over.* Then she would mash wads of banana cake down his throat, slabs of fat bacon, Washington State apples, green pearl strings of peas fresh from the pod, all the things that she was just dying to see him eat. She would grow wilder, she would peg bananas in his ears, stuff Schmierkase up his nose, and work guacamole dip through his hair like ice green styling mousse. Mrs. Fulton fell silent here, as though amazed by her own flight of fancy, but Maria knew exactly what she meant.

That day, as Mrs. Fulton was leaving, she turned to give Maria the first full look of her visit. "It's been a year since the accident," she said. She hesitated a minute, then asked, "You are going to drive again, aren't you?" Maria was silent. Mrs. Fulton continued in a voice of great brightness. "It's really just like being bucked from a horse. There's only one solution—get right back on the big bugger!"

Maria put the rest of the food away. King Bolo whined gently, once. She knelt and put her chin on the top of his head. His fur smelled fresh and sweet, like a clean child.

She read in their bedroom while Bolo kissed her foot, her ankle. Maria liked biographies. She had a particular fondness for famous people who never did a thing until they were forty, or older. Ulysses S. Grant was good; everyone thought he was a bum until he was well into middle age. Grandma Moses was even better. She rarely took up a brush until her seventies, and then what beautiful work she did. Maria had not painted since the accident, and now she bent over the little reproductions of Grandma Moses's paintings. She loved those little winter skaters. On the overleaf was a glowing, consoling summer landscape, lavish summer-afternoon sunshine that warmed you through.

She was not surprised, after an hour or so, to hear stirrings in the kitchen. Jeremy's headaches did not affect his appetite for long. In fact, he had once eaten an entire Thanksgiving dinner, including green apple pie and a great slab of reeking Stilton, while in the grip of what he said was encephalitis. He was, however, delicately critical of Maria eating. Without precisely saying so, he made it clear that she ate too much, or at the wrong time, or the wrong thing. He implied that she was a martyr to sweaty peasant appetites. And yet she knew, and he knew she knew, that he ate a great deal, although in secret. Supplies melted away between midnight and dawn. Sometimes she went down and caught him up to his armpits in herring jars, cracker boxes, marinated mushrooms, with crumbs of feta cheese and Havarti on his lips. And he was furious to be caught. She knew it. He reminded her of certain savage tribes, the ones who believed you stole their souls by taking a picture of them.

Idly, she switched the bedside lamp from high to medium to low, and then back again. The base of the lamp consisted of a pottery model of T.S. Eliot's head. It had been given to Jeremy by one of his students, a girl named Holly. She was the star of his Eliot seminar. She was also twenty-two and had the slim arms, the round baby face of French screen sirens of the thirties. She smelled of sunny flowers, like daisies and jonquils.

Of course, Maria understood that Jeremy needed to spend much more time with Holly, who was his research assistant, since his fantastic discovery of the year before. For Jeremy had accomplished a stunning coup, and in the scholarly world now stood bathed in double rainbows. He had managed to unearth the lost pornographic verses that T.S. Eliot had written in his (somehow extraordinarily hard to imagine) horny young manhood, the randy saga of King Bolo. It was like an opium dream: Jeremy burrowing inch by inch through the mouldering attic of the seaside resort where Eliot had spent his twenty-second summer, the lunatic crone innkeeper mumbling some wild tale of her own grandmother hiding his "dirty, sinful poems"; a little humpbacked trunk, the lock had to be broken, and then Jeremy's head swarming with golden lucky strikes as he recognized the incisive Italianate hand covering pages and pages. What with faded ink, dirt and mold it was close to impossible to read, but he was now deciphering the manuscript, with Holly's help. Nothing had yet been published, but everyone *knew*. One was fawned on at faculty parties. Although Eliot was not quite the towering emperor he once had been, there was already a brisk, though very secretive, bidding war on his juvenile porn. Great chunks and slabs of fame, like some rendingly delicious pâté, lay just ahead for Jeremy.

Maria had wanted to make a loving and yet splashy gesture to applaud her husband. And so she'd bought a gorgeous collie, named him King Bolo, and presented him to Jeremy. Jeremy was mildly pleased, until it became clear that Bolo had already given himself body and doggy soul to Maria. Jeremy dismissed this incomprehensible preference with the remark, "Well, he is a dumb beast, after all," and henceforth ignored him.

Downstairs, Jeremy stirred again. He was preparing to tape music from his favorite rock n' roll nostalgia station, as he did every Friday night. For this one task, he ignored modern technology and recorded the music as he had at fifteen. Jeremy was not only brilliant and profound, he was funky. He had over a thousand tapes and cross-indexed them meticulously. On numerous Friday evenings, Maria had watched his face, which was long-nosed, pale, and ascetic, like a Plantagenet bowman, and wondered what he made of this music, which was all about consuming passions. There were songs about fine, fine boys, and a girl with a pretty face who smelled of Chantilly Lace, crazy arms, the ten commandments of love, and so many others that were all about young, greased-up, hot, human emotions. Lately Maria had often thought that Jeremy had, romantically, the temperament of a conger eel, and so she wondered.

She had also been baffled by a recent discovery. In his very bottommost bureau drawer was a magazine, printed on luxurious paper, called the Sexploits Jamboree. It was carefully hidden under a leather case containing his various degrees and awards. Maria felt as one would upon suddenly discovering that one's housemate of several years has a sixth toe. *But that's just it,* she thought, *remembering some scrap of folk wisdom from her youth. If you have a funny foot, you need a funny shoe.*

She was drawn downstairs when she heard the disc jockey announce that he would soon play Wilson Pickett's version of "In the Midnight Hour." She'd discovered the old song plumb in the middle of her college years, and she associated it with dancing, beatific and stoned, at parties; with riding recklessly on her motorcycle; all-night vigils, wakes, and riots, retreating always at dawn to the arms of Jeremy, her safe, clever, handsome friend. Jeremy at twenty-four looked like Michelangelo's David from the side; he had the virility of a Mongol horde and could charm the pants off a snake. He would always say, "What have you been doing?" She would tell him. He would smoke a cigarette as she talked, looking at her with the grey-green eyes that always reminded her of rocks or water. He would say in a perfectly neutral voice, "My, you are a dark, Lawrencian, life-flows sort of woman, aren't you?" He said it every time, as though it were a private joke between them. She'd read some D.H. Lawrence, but she didn't really understand the reference. It seemed important, though, that he shouldn't know. She would just smile, enigmatically. Then he would throw his cigarette away and they'd make truly astonishing love.

There was also the night she'd brought him *Coven*, the painting that won all those prizes. The canvas measured six feet by six feet and she couldn't imagine, now, how she had carried it all the way to his apartment. She put her cheek beside his, to wake him. She noticed again that his face, whose lines were so classical and severe, smelled innocently of soap. He looked at the painting for a long time, pausing once to put his finger silently on the central white-faced, black-haired warlock. Finally he said, "You are quite something, aren't you?"

"Yes," she said. He was taking her boots off when he suddenly looked up.

"The Whittaker," he breathed, in an absurdly groveling and reverential tone. The Whittaker was the fat prize the Art Department gave to its best student artist. Jeremy clasped her empty boots to his bosom and kissed them passionately, while she knotted her hands in his black warlock's hair and laughed and laughed.

The lyrics of the old song reminded her of those times. *I'm going to wait till the midnight hour, when my love comes tumbling by . . .* "Jeremy?" she said, as she walked into the living room.

"What?"

"When they play 'In the Midnight Hour'—be sure to record it, all right?"

"What?"

She repeated herself, stumblingly. "You will be sure to record it?"

"Oh, I suppose so." He began fine-tuning dials. He said nothing more, but the set of his neck, the faint twist of his mouth, made it clear that her taste for "In The Midnight Hour" was, fatally, what one would have expected.

She retreated to the kitchen. The kitchen was her favorite room, and she had always known exactly what she wanted it to be like. It was all in a painting she had once seen. There should be aunts in calico aprons slicing great boulders of rye bread, a calico cat asleep on the rag rug, turkeys being inserted in the gleaming and beautiful iron stove. Most important of all, children, little weisenheimers in red smocks or overalls, with great plummy squares of gingerbread in their hands. However, she had no relatives whom Jeremy would allow to enter the house, they had no children, and he was allergic to cat fur. She comforted herself with an immense pressed-back rocker of golden wood, which she drew close to the stove. The rocker, at least, was just right. She was about to sit down when she noticed Jeremy's jacket slung across the back. She lifted it up to put it in the closet, and then stood still, with daisies and jonquils and other sweet meadow scents swirling around her.

She decided suddenly to have a bath, a hot, hot one. While the tub was filling, she stood and looked at the container of Roger & Gallet soaps. "Let me see, who is the real Maria today? Jasmine, fern, or orchid?" She chose the fern-scented soap. She looked in the mirror while she was putting her hair in a plastic cap, and for a moment hardly recognized herself. She suddenly remembered a line in a letter Zelda Fitzgerald had written her husband from an insane asylum: *I've got to find someone who can tell me what I was like.*

It was not as though people had not tried to be kind. Someone even sent her an inspirational biography about a paraplegic who made a name for herself painting greeting cards with a brush clenched between her teeth. *But I've got all my arms and legs,* Maria thought. Her right hand had been damaged, but the doctor said it would be completely usable in time. Still, she was disposed to believe that the sender, the anonymous sender, had meant well.

Hugh Grover, one of Jeremy's students, heard that she'd been terribly injured in a car accident, but not that she had survived. He sent Jeremy a very beautiful poem by Ben Jonson, concerning the death of a boy of seven. Evidently, Grover thought that the subject matter was near enough. Jeremy passed it to Maria over her hospital tray, with a smile. "Rather fulsome of Grover. He'll feel like a fool when he realizes you're alive." Grover's later feelings were impossible to guess, since he maintained a huffy silence about the whole matter.

Many people commented on what extraordinary work the doctors had done to mend the damage to her face. Jeremy certainly spared no expense. "We don't want a butcher, after all," he said, and minutely examined the credentials of all the plastic surgeons in the state. Dr. Freitag won the plum. After the operations were over, Jeremy appeared perfectly satisfied. At parties he would put his arm around her shoulders supportively and say in a bright, positive voice, "Don't you think it's amazing what Freitag has done?" Then they would all, Holly and Patrick and the others, turn and stare at her, as though her face were a small oil painting of doubtful provenance and they were examining it for inauthentic strokes, slips of the palette knife. Maria had read somewhere that Picasso looked at things that way, a gaze so intense that it actually seemed to pull the soul of the object loose from its moorings, into his clutches.

"Amazing!" Everyone agreed on this, their voices kind. Of course the tiny scars at the hairline, the slight contraction at the grooves of the nose, were inevitable. Freitag was not a god, after all. Jeremy took a keen, clinical interest in describing how her molars had been retrieved from her chin, and her nose from her ear.

At a poetry reading Maria had once heard a young woman cry out, in a voice of blazing emotion, "—*and in that moment I loved your red scars*—" Was that what she was waiting for, she asked herself. For Jeremy to say he loved her red scars?

Jeremy was right. She was a child.

She took a long bath. She heard Bolo snuffling softly at the door and pictured his great golden bulk, always as close to her as he could manage. When an hour had passed, she climbed out of the tub. Somehow she felt an hour was really the outermost limit for baths. She fumbled in the closet for her favorite cotton wrapper. It was blue and white, cut in the kimono shape she liked, and she crawled into it, sighing. Again, she looked in the mirror. Her ruddy face, with the grave blue eyes, looked back. "Well, that's how it is, my dear," she said.

When she went into the living room, Jeremy had gone upstairs to bed. She stood and looked around. He was so fastidious in his personal grooming that the strange, almost simian disorder to which he could reduce a room still amazed her. She began automatically to pick up socks and fruit peels and Bass beer bottles, then stopped. *The hell with it.* King Bolo, who stood on his feet like a Romanov prince, snuffed at some discarded herring in a coffee cup. The herring smelled like a shipwreck three days old, and he backed up with an expression of implacable disdain.

After a minute, Maria went to the card catalogue that Jeremy kept for his tapes. He hadn't recorded "In the Midnight Hour."

She started up the stairs. Some nights there was really nothing to be done but go to bed. Her glance flicked into the kitchen, though, and in the end she went to the cupboard, then to the refrigerator for ice, and fixed herself a gin and tonic in her one Waterford goblet. As she sat in the rocking chair, drinking it, she noticed a sealed envelope on the kitchen counter. This was a query she was sending to the university about a teaching position in the Art Department. It was addressed to Patrick Nelson, the department chairman, who was Jeremy's best friend. It had been on the counter for many days. Suddenly, from one moment to the next, it became a matter of ferocious importance that she send the letter now, at once. She put the glass down and went into Jeremy's study, where he kept his stamps. Bolo's monstrous shadow swarmed over the walls as he followed her. He lay in Jeremy's antique wing chair as she began her search. The stamps were not in their usual place. In the next hour, as she softly opened and closed drawers, unfolded minuscule scraps of paper, and slid her hand into dark corners, she felt a concentration of senses she had never known before. It was as though she could touch, hear, smell like a blind woman. Her search was systematic and cold, and yet she trembled with excitement. In some sense, Jeremy had always been a mystery to her, and she felt that she was about to know him.

She made many discoveries, the least of which was the roll of stamps in a film canister. For one thing, he had a cache of nude art photos of Holly. An upended Holly was pictured clasping her ankles and looking pensively backward through her legs caressed by swirls of mist. A gymnastic, naked Holly sprang in a mighty leapfrog over a birdbath. *That's our birdbath*, Maria thought in astonishment. She looked closely at the pictures and realized they'd all been taken in the backyard. But how was that possible? She thought about it, and then she knew. Jeremy and Holly had been working on his porn oeuvre while Freitag was lifting her face off in the hospital, and redraping it to its poor best advantage.

Maria left the photos where she found them. When she straightened to go upstairs, it was a little notebook she held. Bolo, too, stretched and rose.

A minute later, she stood at the door of their room and looked at Jeremy sleeping. His corona of curly dark hair and slim, muscular torso made him look like a sexy angel, particularly when he was sleeping and you couldn't see the expression of his eyes. She stood there so long that Bolo was baffled. Then she moved into the room, leaving the hall light on. She put the notebook on the bureau, beside Jeremy's cricket bat. Members of the English Department had learned to play the game the summer before. Quietly she took off her robe, chose a dress from the closet, and put it on. She turned on the T.S. Eliot lamp beside the bed. Jeremy thrashed upward and cursed. She sat down on the bed.

"God damn it," he said, "do you realize what time it is? Turn the fucking light off."

"Jeremy," she said, "I know you're sleepy, but pay attention. Tomorrow you'll have to see Patrick about that teaching job I want."

"What?" he said. His eyes were becoming accustomed to the light. Their strange geological color, like rocks or water, darkened with contempt. "You must be insane. You haven't painted or taught for a year. I won't do it."

"I can handle that job on my head," she said, and although she spoke gently, something in her voice made Bolo look up. "And I can paint at the same time."

"How had you planned to do that?" he said, his eyes on her damaged fingers. "With a hook?"

She said nothing for a moment, and then, "See him tomorrow."

"I won't, God damn it," he said, throwing his pillow down and settling his back against it. He was thoroughly awake now, and beginning to enjoy himself. "I know you were a good painter once, but sometimes these things burn out. As for Patrick—I can't influence that job choice—"

"You can," she said.

"Well, I'm sure they want a fresh face." He liked the sound of that, and repeated it: "Yes, a fresh face." His eyes lingered with voluptuous satisfaction on her scars. "Now," he added, a harder edge to his voice, "get the fuck out of *my* face, go downstairs and look at the books with real painters in them, or whatever the hell it is that you do down there." Maria was motionless, then rose.

She turned to take something off the bureau, and he said, "And turn the damn light off. Some of us have to get up and work tomorrow, you know. And," he sighed, putting his fingertips to his temples, "I've got a splitting h——" He never finished the sentence, for Maria, swinging smoothly from her broad shoulders, brought the cricket bat down with a head-splitting crash. His shockingly high screams died as soon as they were uttered. In the silence that followed, Maria sat down on the bed to put her boots on, then turned to look at the man on the pillow.

With one hand, Jeremy turned over and over the glass shards of T.S. Eliot's head, which lay on his chest, and with the other he tremblingly examined his own skull. He could not believe it was untouched. Only Eliot had been shattered.

Maria looked straight into his rock-grey, water-green eyes, which were now all pupil. "See Patrick tomorrow," she said. She reached over to the bureau, got the notebook, opened it, and held it an inch from his eyes. For a moment, he was afraid she was going to mash it in his face. At this range, in the dark room, it took him fully twenty seconds to recognize the pages, although he'd bought the notebook and he and Holly had sweated bullets over it. There were many different versions of an incisive Italianate script, and numerous drafts of scattered verses copied over and over in letters like wee peas, grains of sand. You could read them a thousand times and yet always come to the same conclusion: the verses were being, not deciphered, but devised.

Maria thrust the little notebook in her pocket, still holding his gaze. In her long red dress, with her cloud of black hair, she looked to him like some gaudy executioner. *"Tomorrow,"* she said.

She left the room, and for a second was illuminated in the bright light of the hall. Her hair swirled back from the high bones of her face as she started down the stairs. For the first time since the accident, Jeremy's mind moved to believe what he saw. It was true. He had gotten his money's worth from Freitag. The man had done extraordinary work. *I should have hired a butcher,* Jeremy thought. He lay in bed and listened to the two of them going down the stairs, the solid tread of Maria's boots and the quiet rush that was King Bolo. She stopped in the living room. A long silence followed.

Maria stood and looked at the long rows of tapes. There were hundreds upon hundreds of songs. Some had names that promised, and others had names that begged: "Be My Baby," "Rescue Me," "Don't Be Cruel," "Hurts So Bad." She gathered them up, armful by armful, and threw them in the still smouldering fireplace. Bolo, solid as a lion in the firelight, looked up at her as though he were laughing. She took the car keys, her raincoat and purse, wrapped her hand in the long fur of King Bolo's head, and they left.

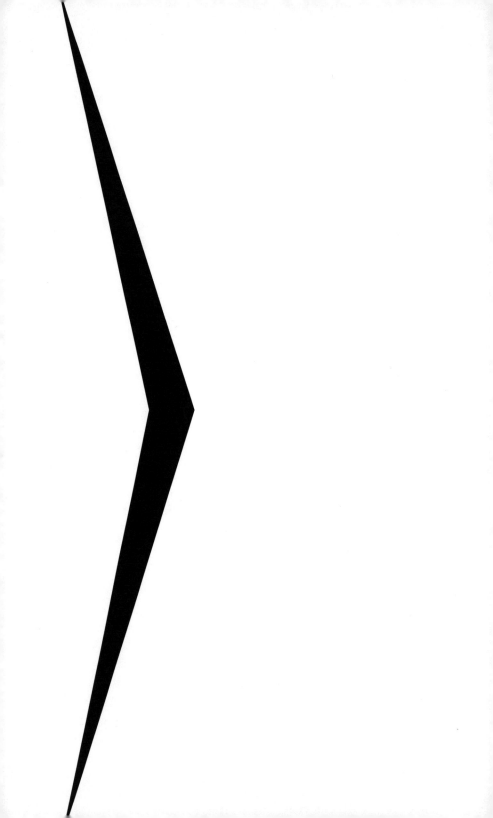

PARTY DOLL

"Lincoln's deathbed physician said he had the body of a Moses. What do I look like, Bill?"

The doctor, who had just finished examining my father, dropped the covers. He said, "You can't put off that quadruple forever."

"Isn't that where you take strips from my ass and sew them to my heart? You keep chopping bits off me, Bill. Christ, what am I going to have left, one nut and my elbow?"

The doctor smiled coldly and put his hat on. "Happy Thanksgiving," he said, and left.

The sick room, the whole house, smelled of turkey and onions. Bernard breathed in slowly. "My seventy-first Turkey Day. Whoopy do." He turned to me, grinning slyly. "Shouldn't you be in the kitchen helping your mother?"

"She isn't my mother," I said, "she's your doxy. She can't be my mother. She's twenty-eight. I'm twenty-nine. Remember?"

My father looked at me with interest. "You almost said that as though you minded."

My mother, my real mother, is sixty. Her name is Josephine. She is so short that my father, during his affectionate years, used to call her Runtkin. She gardens all the time, wearing rump-sprung corduroys—although when caught up in the excitement of the growing season, she's been known to weed at dawn in her nighty. My mother smells of cool ferny soaps, except on the days when she doses her plants with fish emulsion. She reads for hours every night—mostly Shakespeare. She's rarely understood a joke in her life, and my father, who was a stand-up comedian for forty years, said that in the end that was why he divorced her. Actually he was looking for Shirleen, or someone like Shirleen.

Shirleen is my stepmother. Her bulgy curves spring in a nd out under shiny fabrics printed with tiger stripes and jungle flowers. She smells of pe fume with violent police-blotter names: Assault, Love Jump, Drug Delirium. When my father introduced her to me, secretly he lifted his eyebrows and shrugged a little.

"What can I do?" he said to me later. "I like it like that."

My mother took the divorce quite well, although initially she was confused at being told that their marriage was terrible. "I thought it was rather nice," she told me hesitatingly, in her gentle voice. I knew what she meant. She thought it was nice because, to her, the marriage included everything she cared about. First of all there was me, Rochelle. I'm a cartoonist, sometimes even referred to in national publications as "rising." She also included the big garden, the prize legumes with their roots going clear to China. Josephine counted the kitchen, and every meal she and Bernard had shared, from the wedding banquet crown roast and pink Lady Baltimore Cake to the driest heel of rye, old maids in the popcorn pot. She'd thought the marriage had music. She would always listen to the Metropolitan Opera broadcast Saturday afternoons. My father liked jazz, and Coleman Hawkins would cool up the living room around midnight. My mother counted everything, and that is where she went wrong. She mistook her life for her marriage. People do this, but it's the surest way I know to get your face stepped on.

"Hey," I said now to Bernard, craftily shifting ground. "Did I show you the cartoon *New York Magazine* bought?" I reached into my portfolio. "They're asking me if I'll do a series on this couple." I put the drawing in his hand. He studied it silently. The cartoon showed a man and woman in colonial dress. The man was very tall and had my father's face, with a stupid expression. The woman was very short and looked like my mother. She had her hands on her hips and was saying, "Well, one thing I know for sure, Bud. From my heart will grow a red, red rose, and from yours, a briar."

Bernard, whose nickname is Bud, looked stone-faced at the cartoon for a long minute. Then he gave his short, harsh laugh. He always laughed this way at my cartoons, grudgingly, as though the laughter had been extorted from him with menaces.

"Right," he said, "and from my back will grow the knives you keep planting in it. I sent you to that fancy art school, and you got good. Good enough to humiliate me nationally. Hell, you're a gifted little shit. Maybe someday you'll humiliate me internationally."

"It's what I aim toward," I said. "But cheer up. Think of it this way: If I'm good, at least you got your money's worth from the art school."

"Oh, did I?" he said, staring at the cartoon in his hand. "Right. What a sweet deal for me." There was a pause, and then he said, "I'm a little surprised you decided to spend Thanksgiving with the old goat and his doxy."

"Mother said she wasn't going to celebrate Thanksgiving this year."

There was a silence, during which we both visualized Thanksgiving the year before. Josephine had been up at dawn, stuffing a turkey the size of a pony and filling the house with bouquets, some in old milk bottles and blue quart jars and others in Waterford goblets.

In one instant the memory turned us both furious, short of breath.

"You blame me," my father said, "God damn it."

"I blame you because you're to blame. You *evicted* her——"

"It was better not to drag it out. Sometimes it's necessary to be cruel to be kind——"

"This whole concept of necessary cruelty really fascinates me. Take this year." I spoke in a soft, innocent voice, as though I couldn't taste smoking chunks of his guilty heart. "When you half-killed Mom by shoving her out of her own home, it was really all for her own good. Silly old Mom, if only she'd known."

"That apartment is a palace, she's living like a queen, I'm paying a fucking fortune—" By this time he was yelling, climbing out of bed and waving his cane. I knew he wouldn't hit me, he never had. "You're lying," he shouted. "You're lying like a rug," and as I dodged the cane without effort, I studied the eggplant-purple of his face. I always could jump-start the old man into near insanity. On the other hand, I didn't want him to drop dead on me. I held my hand up in a truce. Gasping, he collapsed back on his pillow. For a full minute, there was no sound in the room except my father mastering his breath. He made no attempt whatsoever hide his terribly working face. His eyes were fixed on me, and neither of us blinked. Finally he spoke.

"Go ahead, pour it out, swill it all over me," he assumed a weary burlesque of my face and tone, a sniveling snot-nosed crybaby. "How I *faaa-iled* you and *faaa-iled* your mother and flushed her whole life down the toilet. Well, you know what? Things are tough all around. Personally, I like having a wife who doesn't wander around outside in her nightie talking to herself—"

"Your property has a wall around it, nobody saw her! She was wearing that flannel granny gown, it covers her from head to toe, and she was reciting sonnets from Shakespeare—"

"Well, whatever," he said. "It gave me the creeps. Then there was always the God damned second cousin hanging around. Who ever asked him? I never did."

"Edward has been her best friend all her life," I said.

"Jesus Christ, what could be more pathetic than that? The truth is, I'm happy now, and she could be happy if she tried. She *refuses*."

I said, "You talk about her as if she's some old cow who won't let her milk down."

He smiled slightly and spread his hands, as though to say, *I wouldn't have put it quite that way, but...*

Silently, I tried to calculate words so severe, so cruel, so true, that they would pierce right through the fat over his heart. I said quietly, "She's drinking."

The Thanksgiving table held the smallest turkey I've ever seen, a bowl of bananas, and some dry-roasted nuts. There was also a vegetable salad made from baby carrots, new potatoes about as big as the ball of your thumb, weeny onions, and embryonic beans.

"Oh," said Bernard, "tiny food." His fingers played with a goblet, which held a prudent sufficiency of ice water. Shirleen was drinking orange juice. We did not look at each other, but privately, I shrieked with malicious glee.

For holidays, my mother would provide a sort of pig-out for Renaissance kings. She liked to roast game to a crackling dark gold and surround it with spiced fruits and nuts. She never bothered with vegetables. Bernard didn't like them. In front of her would be a great tart like a wheel, the sweet purple bellies of the plums drifted with cream. Here and there were squat witch's bottles of wine she'd made, and close to my father, a field of cheeses, from the tender brick whose crumbs a baby might enjoy to the unspeakable Tomme de Chevre, his favorite, removed from the others, reeking happily away like a billy goat under its glass hood. (Bernard sighed, and I knew he was thinking of the stink cheese.) My mother's goal for holiday meals was simply to provide your heart's desire. She was shy and mostly silent, but she understood how to make life sweet. In her own métier, she was queen of the court of pleasure.

"Pardon me if I'm wrong," Bernard said now, "but I thought it was Thanksgiving, not Ash Wednesday."

Shirleen carved the turkey. I had to admit she did it neatly. My father told a joke, only twenty years out of date ("Did you hear that Jim Bakker and Jimmy Swaggart are making a movie? It's called *Children of a Looser God*,") and began to cheer up. Shirleen bent over him, spooning green beans and onions on his plate. My father watched her, his nostrils flaring to the force-field of jasmine and tuberose which surrounded her. Suddenly his face looked less like an angry spud. He put his arms around her hips.

I got up, stalked to the sideboard, and filled a big wine glass. I drank most of it on the spot. I brought the bottle back to the table. Shirleen and my father watched me, but said nothing. I lifted my glass to them. "It's because of your newlywed antics," I said. "I have to drink, or puke."

Shirleen opened her mouth to say something, but my father put his hand on her arm. It was then I knew for sure, I knew how guilty he felt about Josephine. I gloated over the knowledge, tasting it as though it were the fattest pink peach in the world. The old man wanted me to approve of Shirleen, of the marriage. He wanted my blessing. Dream on, I thought.

I finished my wine with a flourish, smacking my lips, and poured more, and just then we heard a knock. Bernard and I both jumped in our chairs. The pearl onions on his lips suddenly looked like bubbles from a death gasp.

"Your mother?" He looked so afraid I almost felt sorry for him.

"She wouldn't knock at her own front door," I said. "It's got to be Edward. You know he always comes to Thanksgiving dinner."

"She didn't tell him—"

"He's been in England for eight months. She must not have been in touch—" As my father cursed softly, I stood up, walked to the door, and flung it open. "Come in, Edward!" I said brightly. "We're having gobs of fun!"

My mother's second cousin walked in. Westons are short, but they are built with a powerful compactness. Edward's presence was added to by the thick and flowing tweed coat he wore from September to May.

Edward looked at Shirleen with bewilderment.

"Where's Joey?" he said.

Explanations were awkward. Edward said nothing while they were going on, although the quality of his silence changed. I think he really didn't understand what I was saying at first, and when he did, he immediately turned and looked at Shirleen from

head to foot with intense astonishment. Somehow, his naked in-
credulity was more insulting than if he'd flung banknotes in her
face and shouted "Floozy!" But no matter how bleak his glare, or
mine, there she stood, planted on her big spike heels.

I seated Edward at the table by pressing down hard on his
shoulders. Dinner proceeded. Bernard sensed a little social awk-
wardness at the table, and smoothed it over in his usual way,
asking his guests why the midget was thrown out of the nudist
colony, and what the blind man said when he passed the fish
shop. Shirleen heroically laughed very hard, and was moved to
bring up her own favorite, an ancient subversive one-liner that
probably went back to Mrs. Noah—"'This is going to be great,'
the jackrabbit boasted to his girl, 'wasn't it?'"—at which I too
laughed very hard, Bernard and Edward somewhat less.

I sloshed wine in Edward's and my glasses. "I helped her
bottle this," he said. "Let's see how it turned out." He took a
mouthful of the purplish-red plum, and looked up with somber
pleasure. "A wine with shoulders," he said, using one of Josephine's favorite expressions.

I turned to address Shirleen's expression of stupefied bore-
dom. "He knows everything about wine," I said. "And everything about books. He's a professor of comparative literature.
He speaks several languages."

"Yeah," my father whispered hoarsely to Shirleen, "he's tri-
lingual, he speaks French, German, and Bullshit."

Edward turned to me and said quietly, "Where is she?"

"With her sisters."

"But she's always hated them."

There was nothing to say to this. I drank. Gradually, I was
overcome by a mad, secret hilarity. I could have shrieked with
laughter at the oddity of these three brought together around the
Thanksgiving table. There was Shirleen, with her burly bronze
hairdo, a gelled surfer's wave cresting high over her brow. She
wore a red star dress, as smooth and tight as the head of a drum.
Edward wore his "good" suit, a bombproof woolen imported

from England. He and my mother had been raised together by her Anglophile parents on a Westchester estate. They'd been trained to be passionate readers, gardeners, wine-tasters, and dead shots. Mother said they'd been raised according to the English country code: "If it doesn't move, prune it. If it does move, shoot it."

Bernard's big, high features were flushed red, although he'd been drinking only water. He was wearing a silk dressing gown, a sultan's robe, stunning and gorgeous. Shirleen had given it to him. Every color you could want was in that robe, and as I looked at all those shades of sweet fruit and soft wine, I felt my forehead too turn purple and my blood turn black. I couldn't stand to see my father packaged in her silk. The very sight of the two of them together made me sweat with detestation. Josephine had probably spent the day sitting alone, finishing her own bottle of the wine with shoulders by herself, and that thought from one moment to the next became intolerable. Just at that instant, the front door opened and my mother walked in.

On this freezing day, Josephine wore for a coat only her gardening jacket. Tears of cold stood in her eyes, and her hands were mottled red. "Rochelle," she said, and stumbled around the table to hug me. She smelled of the winter day, her ferny soap, and wine. Edward was already on his feet. They looked at each other for a long moment, and then she turned to face Bernard. Although she held onto a chair back to steady herself, her voice and diction were clear.

"There's this problem of what to do with old women," she said. "Some of them live happily with their old husbands until they die. But some of them are like me." She shook her head, and continued in a tone of astonished protest. "Did you know, did you know that some women are so desperate they even hire surgeons to cut and re-arrange their old bodies?"

My father began to stand up. Edward said, "Sit down." To my surprise Bernard did sit down. He listened, poker-faced, as my mother continued.

"Those who don't want to be anatomized while they're still alive will at least look for magic body-fluffing cream. They search and search. They don't eat what they want, they wear undergarments that cut them in half. I did. They just want their old man to still like them. It doesn't seem like too much to ask, but Bernard thought it was." She looked at me. "You remember, Rochelle, when we talked about mercy killing? You said you were against anything a man might do to a woman that made it necessary to identify her by her dental records. I wonder how Bernard would identify me now?" She opened her purse, took out a handgun and calmly sighted along it. Then everything happened in an instant, Shirleen scrambling over the table to throw her body in front of my father and Edward hurtling toward my mother and Bernard rising and facing her without one word and I had just time to think *he always was a gutty old bastard* and close my eyes when I heard a WHOMP and then a SPLAT and then the strangest sound of all, Edward's laugh.

I opened my eyes. Josephine stood quietly with the gun in her hand. The little turkey carcass had been blasted against the wall and was now sliding to the floor leaving a smear of grease and dressing.

"Well, for Chrissake! Buddy!" Shirleen said. She embraced him and wept.

Bernard patted her shoulder absently, but it was my mother he looked at. He said only, "You wanted to kill me, Jo?"

"If she wanted to kill you," Edward said, "you'd be dead." He reached for the gun. Josephine held on to it tight, and he pried her fingers open. He put the gun in his pocket.

"There's gravy on my ear," Bernard said. "If you hadn't jogged her wrist at the last minute, it would be my brains."

"Oh, for God's sake, Bernard, don't be such a baby," Edward said. "I can't believe a grown man is making this fuss. Why, Joey's father used to test our nerve by shooting apples off our heads. He would have considered a turkey more or less the side of a barn."

My mother said, "I've had such a bad time, Eddie. He hurt me so, and there was nobody—it seemed as though the only way to get back—"

"Hush," he said loudly, speaking over her voice. Then, for the first time I could remember in my whole life, he put his arms around her. "It's over," he said. "Things happened because I was gone. Now I'm back."

Edward wasted no time in getting my mother warm and sober. "Coffee," he said coldly. As Shirleen made it, he swathed Josephine in every cashmere throw and afghan he could find. I had drunk a lot of wine and could hardly make sense of the march of events. Ten minutes before, Josephine had been in despair, icy-fingered, gutted. Now she was a cherished little prize, her rosy face and tumbled curls rising from the most luscious fabrics, the tender belly hairs of royal white goats. Bernard looked at her as though he could hardly believe his eyes. Edward stood over her while she drank the coffee, every drop. He put his hand to her flushed cheeks and brow to make sure she was warm. Then, imperiously, he stripped the afghans away, letting them lie where they fell. He wrapped her up in his big old woolly coat and buttoned it right up to her chin. She looked like a darling little bear. He wrapped his six-foot muffler around her. He put his heavy gauntleted gloves on her little hands.

Josephine turned to me and put her arms around me. "Come see me tomorrow," she said. "I'll be at Eddie's."

Bernard and Edward exchanged their last words.

"Hot Springs tonight, hey?" said my father. "Well, it only took you forty years."

"I always detested you, Bernard," Edward said.

"Oh, that's all right. I always detested you too."

"I guess this means we won't have to spend Thanksgiving together anymore."

"I guess not."

Edward said to me, "See you tomorrow, Rochelle."

I grabbed a wine glass off the table and lifted it to him.

In the hall, Josephine noticed Bernard's fine long scarf hanging from the hat-tree. She pulled it off and put it around Edward's neck. Then she turned to go outside. As she walked past Bernard, he said, "Try not to blow anybody's head off on the way home."

"Yeah," Shirleen chimed in supportively, "don't whack anybody unless it's absolutely necessary!"

Edward stopped dead in the doorway. He said to Josephine, "What's that quote I'm thinking of—you know, Omar Khayyam—something about hounds, curs—"

"'Dogs bark,'" Josephine said clearly, "'but the caravan passes on.'"

Regally, they flung their mufflers about themselves and departed.

After the door closed, I wasn't sure what to do. It seemed as though everyone had already used the best lines and exits. Shirleen had disappeared into the kitchen. My father got a sponge and began cleaning the turkey off the wall and floor. I was surprised at his calmness, until I remembered some of the places he'd worked. I sat down close to him. I watched him for awhile, and then I said, "You really are the most awful man."

"An awful man? Why? We were happy for a long time. Runtkin and I—" he fell silent, and after a minute pegged the sponge into the bucket. "Besides, I never said I was running for Pope."

Just at that moment, Shirleen shouted from the kitchen. "Rochelle!" Her voice held some quality that made the short hairs on my neck stand up.

Shirleen was standing at the kitchen table, my open portfolio before her, looking at a cartoon. It showed a strange couple at an auto showroom. The man was a mass of decay with my father's face. The woman was an infected-looking wench, wearing practically nothing, with Shirleen's face. The car salesman pointed toward a superb old Mercedes, whose quality, in every nut and bolt, produced a visible shimmer around it. I'd given the Mercedes my mother's face, with tears on the hood. The disgusting husband was saying, "But I don't want some dumpy old classic! I want a ride that's *fly* and *baa-aaad!*"

We both stood there looking at the cartoon. After a long moment, Shirleen closed the portfolio. She said, "What do you think I am?"

I wasn't quite drunk enough to say *Whore*. So I said, "You're a party doll."

"*What?*"

"You were on the cover of *Vixen*."

"*Vixen?* Hell, I was on the cover of *Players*. So what? They're just pictures." She spoke in honest puzzlement. Her serious eyes confused me. She said, "Did you think I was a hooker? I was a model, very successful. I did a hundred of those covers."

"Doesn't it bother you that maybe twenty million people in this country know what you look like with your clothes off?"

"Give me a break!" she said. "It's like I said, they were just pictures. Just a job. As for twenty million people, big deal. I look good with my clothes off. I eat right, I exercise hard. I'm not ashamed of it."

"But those magazines—the shurroundings—" The wine, or my confusion, slurred my words. I tried again. "Like, what did your job *involve*?"

"Oh," she said, "you mean the editors, the photographers? No, they never dared. I would have broken anybody's arm who tried. Well, wait a minute." She thought. "There was just one photographer, near the beginning. He said he was arranging my pose, but he grabbed a handful. I hit him just once," and she raised her strapping right arm, the hard blue jewels of her eyes on me, "and he bounced off every wall in the studio. I lifted him off the floor by his hair, I slammed him up against the door, I looked him in the eye and I said, 'Don't touch me. Don't *think* about touching me. Don't touch yourself and *pretend* it's me. Nothing!'" She opened her hands suddenly and I seemed to see the photographer sag to the floor, a few of his moussed curls drifting down after him. "Then I stood over him and said, 'Because if you do, I'll bash in your ugly little face, you'll be looking for your rib cage up a tree, do you understand what I'm saying?' He never bothered me again."

"I believe you," I said.

She was silent for a minute. With astonishment I saw tears forming in her eyes. She said, "You called me a party doll. So that's what you thought of me. You thought that before I met Buddy I lived like a pig, did everything bad." I opened my mouth, then shut it. She said, "My parents raised me very strict. For two years after I graduated high school, I was secretary to a priest. I can type!" Bitterly, she reflected on my two fatal words. "Party doll? I washed that floor you're standing on. I cooked that food in your belly. I know you laugh at my food, you think," her cheeks flamed, "that your mother made such great food. Well, your mother's food almost put Buddy in the ground. Fat and sugar are like poison to him; she just never thought, she poured it all over him like toxic waste. Now, I've made up my mind to *save him*," she pronounced the words proudly, "and I'm *going to*, and you sneer at me for trying."

"No," I mumbled, "that is—"

She said, "I just want to say one thing about my life before I met Buddy. He was not my first man, but he was my last. That is all any reasonable man can ask."

In the living room, I put my coat on. My father said, "You and Shirleen talked—?"

"Yeah."

After a minute he said, "I want you to know I didn't realize your mother minded so much. About the divorce, I mean." I said nothing. The stubborn old spud of Bernard's face looked as hard as ever, but his eyes simmered with the same demand I'd seen all day. *Bless Shirleen and me, damn you! Bless us!*

Those goofy Romeo eyes were so young I could hardly stand to look at them. It came to me suddenly that, before my father met Shirleen, his eyes looked like sea-stones.

PRIZES

Garrett Palmer was the sexiest poet that year. When a poet wins a big prize, his wit is sweeter to everyone, his shoulders seem more muscular. He has more hair, and it curls.

When Garrett walked into the hall where the reading was to be held, there was a halo effect around his hair, and people ate up his famously funky leather jacket as though it were a sacred cloak of monkey fur and auk feathers worn by an Aztec prince. True, some of the faces watching him were shriveled by envy. Possibly because so many poets have obscenely wretched early lives and serve as the hunchbacks of their various parochial schools and girl scout troups, they tend to be lacerated people who are deeply fascinated by prizes and all forms of public awards and acclaim. It seems to them that all the glitter and soft licks should do something to heal. However, you could massage them slowly with vats of goose grease, pin medals as big as trash can lids on their narrow bowed chests, and it would not help. Nothing could, because their ills are irremediable.

I've had time to ponder this because I'm a poet, and also because of my junior position in the department. I do workhorse duty at the readings. I buy the white wine, oversee disposal of the folding chairs, serve as walker to visiting foreign dignitary poets and local dipsomaniac poets. I investigate reports of smoke in the can and throw out freshman poets sneaking butts.

Garrett Palmer had won the Pinehurst. As I say, he shone and glowed in our eyes, but not everyone felt that way.

"God, I hate that smug son of a bitch," Jimmy Danaan said. Danaan had dug in by the wine. He too was dressed in leather, but the effect was far different. Not for the first time, I reflected that he was lucky he had a teaching load that would drop a moose. The chairman had wanted to drop-kick Jimmy out for many years. But Jimmy was safe as long as he held up the department on his chunky little cement block shoulders. Right now he was pouting because he'd been forbidden to read. I secretly felt the chairman had overreacted to Jimmy's high-spirited pretense of mooning the audience at the last reading. After all, Jimmy's ancient teaching corduroys were so baggy he went around in a sort of permanent half-moon anyway.

"You're drunk," I said.

"Nonsense," Danaan said grandly. At this point, he spotted Molly Blevek and began shouting to her. "Ah, a fleshy girl in a pink angora sweater. Bring some of that over here, mama. Jeezez, Janey, look at the lovely fat can on her, the kind that makes a man want to plant his boot in it, a truly queenly butt. Yet she walks like Bambi. And here she is."

Molly pushed him away, hard. "Don't you know that in this crowd you can get murdered for talking that way? You're a fat, drunken, stupid man and you will never, ever get tenure." In spite of her cold looks and hard words, there was something in her voice, and in his gaze, that told me they'd recently been to bed together, and had been well pleased with each other when they got there.

He tucked his big red face in her shoulder, and they stood like that for a minute. The two of them looked like Beauty and the Irish Beast. He was silent for a few beats, eyes closed, then began softly singing rock lyrics, *'I'm in my prime for tearing it up . . . I just can't tear it up enuff!'* and then random mumbles from a song I didn't know, *'sweetest piece of lovin' any girl ever had . . .'*

She tried to look coldly disgusted, but her face was not made for that expression. A delicate flush grew and sat on the oval of her cheeks. He turned down the turtleneck of her sweater to kiss her neck, and his adoring eyes suddenly bulged crazily. "Jesus, Mary, and Joseph, where did you get those? I'm in my little room writing sonnets to you, and you're out fucking about like Madonna and Catherine the Great and all those raving historical sluts?"

Certainly she did have enormous hickies, I had never seen any so big and black, they looked almost like a failed garroting attempt.

"Christ, woman, whom have you been dating, Vlad the Impaler?"

"*Shut up,*" Molly said, showing him her fist. At this moment, Garrett Palmer reached our group.

Nothing succeeds like success, as the saying goes, and Garrett had looked pretty good to begin with. Now we accorded him the attention we might have given a strolling sun god. He was a tall, broad-shouldered man with fresh skin and a full head of romantically tumbling hyacinthine curls, jet black. He looked like an extremely sexy and effective young pharaoh. He had java-black eyes, which noticed everything, and now t hey fell on Danaan, who was filling his big coffee thermos at the wine bowl. "Topping up your Maxwell House?" Palmer said with a smile.

Danaan, who spent his life moving seamlessly from one luridly inappropriate emotion to the next, stood with the dripping thermos in his hand and grinned at Palmer. The effect of his crooked teeth through his stubbly beard was not pleasant. "Congratulations on getting the Pinery Boy award, Garrett," he said. "Oh, excuse me, of course I meant, the Pinehurst."

"*Pinery Boy?*" Garrett repeated with a baffled smile.

"Yes, because," said Danaan, taking a big snort out of the thermos, "we could all see the log-rolling from here."

I was secretly delighted that this had been said, but that I had not been the one to say it.

Garrett, who beneath his smooth exterior is the toughest son of a bitch you will ever meet, laughed handsomely. "And that's your disinterested opinion, is it?"

"It is."

"Well, I'm surprised you didn't win some kind of prize or other yourself. You write the kind of huge, gassy—excuse me," he corrected himself, "of course I meant, bravura pieces that often win prizes."

"Yes, and so I would," said Danaan, picking up a cock-tail weiner on a toothpick and staring at it sadly, "but in college I didn't belong to a fraternity, and I didn't have any asshole fraternity brothers, and now when I enter contests, there's no old fraternity-brother-judge-asshole to remember Jimmy Danaan."

Now, Garrett did not publicize it, but in his college days fifteen years before he'd been a Deke, and so had the president of the Pinehurst panel. They'd swung many a stein together. Garrett laughed heartily at Jimmy's remark, showing all of his fine teeth. "No, I guess there wouldn't be many to remember you, would there? You were pretty much an outcast at Bogtrot U., or wherever the hell it is that you went, from what I've heard. Damn, Jimmy, you should have pledged when you had the chance."

Now those shining black eyes fastened on Jimmy's cocktail weiner. He gestured toward it, and spoke solicitously. "Christ, you shouldn't have so many of those. They'll clog you all up. In fact, as a friend, I would have to tell you that you look terrible. What do you live on, ham fat? Look at that." He pointed to Danaan's paunch, which gleamed whitely between gaping leathers. "What the hell is that? Are you hiding a Vietnamese pot-bellied pig in your jacket?"

Danaan put his hands on his stomach and smiled beatifically. "This is my beer gut, Garrett. Women admire it. After all, as a friend told me recently," he looked into Molly's eyes with a smile, "a fine machine needs a big shed."

Garrett looked disconcerted, but only for a second. Then he said, "Oh, do you find that so?" He put one hand on his own flat stomach and the other around Molly Blevek's shoulders. "I never did."

The sight of Jimmy Danaan's neck suddenly swelling like a cobra's hood recalled me to my duties. "Come on, Garrett and Molly, it's almost show time and we still have to plan the line-up. Zenna Freitag is such a wreck with stagefright she wants to be first and get it over with. Bill Keller is going to do poems from his llama book and is going to be in costume, and there's some new kid who's been nagging me—"

This last was Molly's fault. She had persistent delusions of democracy, and insisted that a student unknown should be allowed to finish every reading. Her idea was that some infant Rimbaud would be heartened by the audience's adulation. Of course, what they saw was the audience's asses moving away from them and out the door.

When I got Garrett away from Danaan I said, "Don't mind Jimmy."

"Why would I mind Jimmy?" Garrett said. "He keeps my edge up." Then he added something unexpected. "Most people don't know they're alive. At least he knows."

Eventually the reading began. Zenna Freitag exhausted the audience with her stagefright. Bill Keller's llama costume was a big hit, particularly the udder, which he waggled sensuously during the meatier portions of his poem about Buddy, Buster, and Emanuelle. Molly Blevek did chaste, severe political poems without adjectives, which made people feel guilty about noticing her gorgeous shape. As for Garrett, he liked the plum spot, second to the last, where he more or less mopped up the gravy in terms of audience response. Really, most of us didn't even envy the guy. It seemed beside the point somehow. He was so smart, so gifted, and he looked so good.

Jimmy Danaan drank steadily through Freitag's hysterics, Keller's sore teats, Molly's professed solidarity with the Aleut. He did mumble, "Send them your pink angora sweater, it's cold up there," but not very loud, and people were able to ignore it.

When Garrett stood to read, his students leaped up all over the room and trooped down front to sit at his feet. This was their habitual tribute to the master. It was probably against the fire laws, but it warmed people's hearts, so I let them be. Garrett was such a popular teacher that he even had a couple athletes in his class. I noticed Sam Rugoski with his shoulders as big as a

Gothic church door and his almost white brush cut bristling fiercely above his big square head. Garrett began, "I'll be reading from my new book, *I Speak Tiger*—"

"Actually," Danaan remarked to his neighbors, "that should be *I Speak Stupid*."

Rugoski shifted himself massively to glare at Jimmy, and there was a rustle, but it passed, and that was the last we heard from Danaan until Garrett had almost finished. The audience was in the kind of swoon he could always induce, which was produced by his burnt-sugar baritone, the exquisitely judged funkiness of his clothes, his glamorous vitality, and even his poems.

"And last of all," Garrett said finally, "something for my love." He then read a poem about Molly so tense, hot, and bold that I privately decided, once and for all, that as a poet, Garrett had a hardball. There had been times in the past when I wondered.

It would have been interesting to hear how the poem ended, but when Garrett reached the part about ravening like a voluptuous viper over the beautiful neck of his love, a sort of pre-history scream blasted from the back of the room. I and the rest of the audience turned to see Jimmy Danaan bounding toward the podium with red demented stoat's eyes, claws out and flexed for Garrett's gullet. Sam Rugoski placed himself between the two of them, and now he looked like a cathedral wall.

There was a period of almost indecipherable confusion when a lot of things happened that I could not do much about. Some people told me later that I should have called the security guard at once, but at the time I thought it was better for Jimmy to try to batter Rugoski rather than our frail, elderly guard. Also, like everybody else, I was stunned that something was actually happening at a reading. There were blows and oaths and kicks, and blood spilled. Jimmy threw up at some point. I think that most people in this audience had never seen sweat, drool, vomit, and blood on the floor separately, let alone together. I will give Danaan credit, there was no quit in the scrappy little bastard at all. Apparently, he never doubted he would eventually dominate

Rugoski, and then murder Garrett. I was watching him briskly roll out from under the big Air Jordan on his neck, relieved that he didn't seem to have spinal injuries, when somebody thumped me hard on the shoulder.

"It's my turn to read now," the new kid said, glaring at me, foamy-mouthed like a rabid dog. "Why aren't you announcing me, you said I could read, Garrett's done, they're all done, it's my turn now!" He frantically shook his mouldering briefcase in my face.

Nothing a student poet could do should surprise me, but I was surprised. "You're crazy," I said. I pointed to Danaan rolling and bucking, as busy as a nest of snakes, Rugoski clamping his hands around Jimmy's throat, and Molly trying to force them apart. I walked rapidly away to call the security guard. The kid followed so closely I thought he had his teeth in my sleeve. "No," he said. "You promised, you said I could read, I follow Garrett, he just finished, I read now."

Although he was small and slight in build, he was wearing some kind of ankle-length, enormously bulky Stalinist storm-coat, fiercely strapped and belted, with commanding epaulets. He always wore this coat, no matter what the weather.

"Oh for Christ's sake," I said, mainly to get him out of my face, "go read."

He did read, after moving the microphone stand a few feet away from the coil of battlers, the blood and vomit. The security guard came. I'd called him to save what was left of Jimmy. There was a lot of milling around. Rugoski was sitting on Jimmy's chest, and Molly was pounding the hell out of Rugoski's back and crying. Jimmy was bleeding from the nose and mouth, bucking furiously as he tried to kick Rugoski in the head. The kid read on, dozens of fiercely scribbled papers dripping from his hands, strutting to and fro, tossing his lank hair.

Garrett had stayed throughout at the side of the melee, like a pitcher saving his arm. I went to stand beside him. With his height, rich coloring, and exaggerated shoulders, he looked like a big, virile archangel bending his powers to observe, for a moment, the measly doings of weasel earthlings. But the expression on his face was deeply attentive. I noted in wonder that he was listening to the kid. In fact, he was the only person in the room listening to the kid. Twice, as the boy finished a poem and flung it to the floor, Garrett bent to pick it up and quietly held it as he listened. I tried to tune in myself for a minute, but could make little sense of what I heard. It was like listening to a profoundly foreign, and unendurably intense, and yet somehow exalted, harangue. It was like trying to make sense of a conflagration.

So I gave it up and watched the security guard prop up Danaan. Jimmy looked as fresh as you might expect of somebody who'd drunk half a gallon of wine and thrown it up, been sat on, kicked in the nose and crotch and had his arms twisted almost out of their sockets. However, he wasn't finished yet, not by a long shot. When the guard accused him of mayhem, Jimmy drew himself up and said in an offended voice, "I did not punch the man in the chest, I was just touching his shirt to see if it was one of those sweatshop imports." Then he was supported from the room with Molly walking beside him, holding his hand. Garrett watched them go. The kid had temporarily stopped reading, because he was searching for a special poem that was, of course, at the very bottom of the hundreds in his bulging briefcase.

I said to Garrett, "I'm sorry about Molly," in a muted voice, letting him know I respected his pain.

"No," he said. "I always knew I wasn't enough of a social service project to keep her interested."

I sighed. Then I said, in a serious voice, "I'm afraid Molly's going to regret this. Jimmy's a *disaster*."

"Oh, do you think so?" said Garrett, looking happier.

Actually, I thought Molly would greatly enjoy being the making of Danaan. She would begin with basic things, like slapping his head off every time he talked dirty in public. She would hold his hand through root canals, frog-march him to AA meetings, throw out his bunion-sprung brogues and rump-sprung corduroys, and buy him pants with a higher rise. She would lure him into bathtubs by climbing in first, then tell him to wash. If he protested, she would smack him silly, ball him senseless, and scrub him like a pot. They were made for each other. They would have a very happy life.

"I can't find it!" the kid suddenly cried out, frantically dumping the contents of his briefcase on the floor. "It's not here, and it was the one poem—"

"Never mind," Garrett said. "You gave a fine reading." The boy flinched back and looked up scowling, in wonder and distrust. He was like some fierce little animal who had never heard a kind word in his life, and could not believe in it when he had. "What's your name?"

"Arnie Rimble," the boy said unwillingly, and a blush flashed all over his homely face. "I know it's a funny name."

"It's not funny," Garrett said. He showed Arnie the poems he held. "When did you write these?"

"This morning. I had second thoughts about the fourteenth stanza in—" and he launched into an explanation so dense, packed, and technical it felt like being hit on the head with a brick, about his second thoughts, and his third thoughts, and his reversals, homages, and sudden revelations. Garrett listened, and then asked questions. I was struck by something new in his manner. If he had been a stranger, I would have called it humility.

They talked for several minutes about the poems, as the room emptied out. Arnie became more and more animated, eyes shining, rubbing his coarse red hair with both hands, punching one fist into the other. His forelimbs sprang into weird, exuberant full-arm gestures. Finally he fell silent, looked down, and again was overcome by ferocious blushes. He said, almost inaudibly, "Does this mean you like my poems? Can I join your class?"

"You don't need my class," Garrett said, and it was the only time in all the years I'd known him that he sounded sad. "You will never need my class at all." As the boy's face began to cloud,

Garrett suddenly thumped the flat of his hand against the bulging greenish chest of the Soviet stormcoat he wore. "It's a compliment, Arnie," he said. "A compliment. But, if you want to, of course you can join."

We helped Arnie pick up the great heap of poems on the floor, and he carefully stowed them away in the ripped briefcase with its crazy strappings of duct tape. There was a pause, then Garrett said, "Are you two hungry? There's that Burger King a block away—"

"I like Whoppers," Arnie offered shyly.

Arnie walked ahead of us out the door. Garrett reached out to lightly touch one of the epaulets on his shoulders. He said to me quietly, "I had a cool coat like that once."

THE WANDERER

I roam around around around around
—Ernie Maresca, "The Wanderer"

He loves them all: orange-haired widows with their T-bill doubloons, diamond-eyed rich girls looking for wild young men. This time he's been gone three months.

I look at Rob's picture on the piano. My brother, who is twenty (I am forty), looks like a young Jerry Lee Lewis. At his last birthday party, he did his Jerry Lee imitation. He took a microphone, mashed it to his face as though he was going to eat it, and snarled "Whole Lotta Shakin'." He sat down at the piano and played a slow riff with one hand while unloosening his tie and undoing all buttons above the waist. He stopped playing, made a purring growl, suddenly reared up, and kicked the piano stool ten feet into the wall. He swarmed over the keyboard and played brilliant glissandos with his feet, his nose, and his hind end, shook his curly yellow hair over his face and with foam at the mouth jumped all the way into "Whole Lotta Shakin'." That was three months ago.

I have a stack of papers to correct, but instead I examine over and over the valentine I got that day. It is just a scrap of construction paper and tinfoil with a few words written on it, but it seems to vibrate in my hands with—malice? Despair? Hysterical misery? I always remind my psychology students that analysis cannot make anyone happy. I make them memorize Freud's exact words to a patient: *Much will be gained if we succeed in transferring your hysterical misery into ordinary human unhappiness.*

What a lodestar of hope, I tell my students, for all you freaks out there.

On the front of the card, Rob has written in his tiny deadeye backhand, "For you, Rose. Your favorite color, red." On the back his handwriting has noticeably fallen apart—after what?—but I decipher the shattered old man's script: "Aren't you going to come? *What will become of me?*"

I'd talked to Augie Bremer about Rob. Some in the department call Bremer a wild old Jungian boar, but if so, he never puts a hoof wrong. He always knows where in the mind's forest to find the most abundant, the sweetest leaves. So as I spoke, he nudged me with his big learned snout in the gentlest way. "Then he said what?" "Then he did what?"

As a family friend, Bremer had known Rob for many years. More than once, I'd surprised a spark of diagnostic fervor in Bremer's eye as he looked at Rob, listened to his conversation. The old truffle-hunter knew, felt in his bones, smelled out a dark pungent lump of delicious pathology. But he had no direct knowledge of Rob's private life. Now, as I told him, his responses were so quiet, so uninflected by censure or shock, that I allowed myself to hope. But when I stopped speaking, he didn't hesitate for a minute. In diagnosis, Bremer is also like an old Civil War surgeon who doesn't believe in waiting to get a patient drunk before neatly severing the gangrenous limb.

He got up and closed the door, although it was a Saturday and the building was empty. Then he sat down at his desk and looked at me. "He's a sociopath," he said calmly. "As you already knew."

After a minute, I said, "Jungians don't use words like sociopath."

"Why do you suppose I closed the door?"

We looked at each other. Finally he continued. "Nothing to be done about it, in terms of medication. If he survives into his thirties, he may simply outgrow it. Some of them do." I looked at this single green leaf, and tried to be content. But Bremer was still thinking, working it out, and he was not satisfied. I could tell by looking at him. There was something more that he felt it his duty to impart.

I tried to forestall him by standing up hastily, turning to leave, but he wouldn't have it. "Rose," he said. I turned back to face him. He said, "I have to say that, in my opinion, he is not one of those who gets better."

"You have to say it?" I said. "Why? You would never say it to any other patient's sister."

"You're one of us," he said. "You can take it." He returned my gaze calmly. Then in a voice of infinite kindness, he said, "You should walk away."

I hardly recognized my own poor whisper: "But he is all—" and although I managed not to say it, the parched little phrase lay between us just the same: *all I have.* Oh, only our most pitiful patients said that. I blundered out of the room somehow. Bremer and I never referred to the conversation again.

Three years before, Mother had said, "You'll have to save Rob now. I'm too tired. And you must always remember that no matter what, he is your baby brother." She made me promise. I would pay his debts. I'd arrange the best rehab for him when he needed it, and he would. I must shield him from retribution, when he'd beaten or robbed someone. Above all, I must never, ever allow events to force him into prison, "because he is too beautiful to go there." Then she received the Last Rites and, ec- static-eyed, running for her life, died. For years she'd been told by every friend she had, "That kid will break your heart." At the funeral, several of them hissed at him, "You broke your mother's heart." One friend did not hiss. Instead, she gathered him up and took him home with her. Since then, he had often changed one over-blown rose for another.

Many times I thought of a folk painting I had seen once that was entitled *The Prodigal Son Revelling and Sweltering with Har- lots.* The Prodigal Son had a jug of corn liquor raised to his lips. Three big eighteenth-century Mae West women were dancing in their shifts, their yellow marcelled hair streaming back horizontally, and swine rooted in the background. They all looked as though they were having a whale of a time. In the Bible, the Prodigal Son's mother and older sister are not mentioned, but it can be assumed their hearts were broken.

Rob was proof against the effects of revelling and sweltering, up to it, his young tough Jerry Lee face didn't go soft. As for the women, no matter how abruptly he left them, robbing them blind, shattering them and their collections of crystal, sneaking out the hour before dawn with his arms full of animal pelts from endangered species, Italian silk around his neck, and stolen jewels in his ears, they never called the police. They wanted him back. They were permanently, as Jerry Lee Lewis said in the song, "Breath-less-ahhh."

I turned the card in my hands, this way and that. It was midnight. I wouldn't be able to sleep anyway, and suddenly I decided that I might as well go. He would be expecting me. I would save him. It would be the eighth time. Sometimes he discussed the different times with me, with an air of discriminating judgment. "Poor Amy, she took it hard, didn't she? Crawling after us on her hands and knees. Although Bethany was definitely the worst. A knife. Who would have thought she had it in her?"

I looked in the mirror. I don't look like Jerry Lee's older sister. I look like what I am, a college psychology teacher, a sort of spinster mandarin. I wear heavy serious clothes in elegant semi-mourning: fine deep blacks, tweed with the texture of a Victorian beard, silk blouses the blameless white of lilies and snowdrops, a touch of mauve at the throat. My big, excellent shoes are made for me in England.

I took off my suit and put on my cat-burglar outfit: black turtleneck and black cords. I changed my pumps for jackboots with steel-toe construction. I brushed my hair for a long time, then whipped it to the top of my head and pinned it in the shape of a coiled snake. I made up my face with care. My personal style icon is Joan Crawford. When I am sick at heart, my bold red Joan Crawford mouth and shoulder pads carry me through.

I outlined my eyes in glamorous kohl. I wondered what I would look like by dawn.

A year before, Bethany had tried to stab me. For a long time I refused to go after him. But he sent me a note: "If I thought you would never save me again, I would kill myself—*really* kill myself. You understand?" What would he say if I sent him a note: "If I thought that you would ever ask me again, I would kill myself— *really* kill myself. You understand?"

I went into Rob's room, his boyhood room, carrying an armful of fine white linen.

At home, he liked everything around him to be white. I made up his narrow bed, which still had the crucifix over it.

Then I drove across town under little evening stars. The velvety night landscape lay softly to my right and left, and I smoked, drawing the smoke in all the way to the thorax and out again into the dark air. I drove slowly through neighborhoods that, by almost imperceptible degrees, grew richer and richer. The streets had the names of ancient aristocratic families: York, Seymour, Leicester. Suddenly there it was, 123 Tudor Lane. I backed into the driveway. More than once, the fast start had been essential. I sat in the car looking at the garden, then up into the sky. It was remarkably clear, and there seemed no reason why I should not sit in the car for a moment. The constellations steamed around overhead.

I stub out the cigarette, draw on my black suede gloves with the long gauntlets. They are not necessary, but Rob has said, "Those gloves are such a nice touch. I love the gloves." I climb out of the car and feel my face changing. I don't know what the new face looks like, but I imagine Jeckyll-and-Hyde convulsions. Still, I have a strange feeling of being unprepared. I have not sufficiently hardened my heart. You never know exactly what will happen on these excursions, but the one thing you will need for sure is a hard heart.

I walk up to the front door, and my boots, which are cut like very elegant jackboots, make not one sound.

I ring the bell. After a moment the door opens. A woman is standing there in a kimono. She looks me up and down, and I see myself as she must, tall and slim as a sword in my blacks. Do I reek of perfidy? No. She doesn't know yet that I am the night raider, so there is a little bewildered welcoming smile on her face. Perhaps Rob told her that his sister was coming over, and she would expect to offer drinks, snacks. She is not ill-looking, if you could just get over your idea of what a human being should look like. She has very big hair, a tottering plutonium beehive. Two months ago, Rob told me in a phone call, "Doreen has this great retro hair." Her make-up has a life of its own. It is a brave and passionate depiction of a young woman of the 1940s, with more colors in her face than an English cottage garden. She has kind blue eyes with shadows the color of passionfruit painted around them. She looks behind herself suddenly in a movement she cannot control, and when she faces me again her eyes carry a torch, and my own fall before them. Her kimono is ravishingly lovely and expensive. It is the sort of nymph's garment that often only an older woman can afford. She is heavy, with the surging geological bosoms that fairy tale illustrations give to witches. Yet I think she is an attractive woman, with those eyes full of un-quenchable life. Her face is changing as our silence stretches on and on. Finally she says, "You've come for Rob."

I walk past her into the living room, which smells sweetly of potpourri. *Money musk*, I think. I look around. My Rob is like a cat; he will have some picked and chosen spot of ultimate comfort. I find him asleep in a daybed around a corner of the L-shaped living room. He is sprawled out, atomic punk prince in his high-tech tennis shoes, his black leather pants, and $500 black Chinese worker's shirt with wine spilled on it. His black eyelashes, his mother's pride, lie on his perfectly shaven tawny cheeks. Rob has always aspired to be wild, burning up in some ultimate crisis of debauchery, but his personal apocalypse would have to nose in between the three well-chosen meals a day, the two serious daily showers. Although he smells of wine—in fact, he probably threw it all over himself, hoping to impress me with the reek of delirium—his clean, well-groomed young man's scent is uppermost.

Doreen comes to stand beside me. We stand shoulder to shoulder like matey old sisters, the suet of her upper arm against mine, and watch him sleep. Then his eyes open, and at first they look at me vaguely through a hemp-brown haze. Slowly, the fog clears. He says, "I knew you'd come." There is such triumph, such satisfaction in his voice. He ignores Doreen. Everything in his posture is light and powerful as he stands up and walks to a big cupboard. He fumbles behind blankets and pulls out a valise. This will contain the cream of his clothing, beautifully wrapped in tissue paper, and any of her possessions that are sufficiently small, dense, and perfect.

"I'm ready," he says. "Let's go." I hear beside me an eerie choking moan. It sounds like a wolf with an arrow down its throat. I do not want to look at Doreen. I don't want to have to remember what she looks like at this moment. But last year, Marcy was able to jump me and claw me because I turned my back to her, and so I face Doreen. She backs slowly until she stands dead center before the front door, the folds of her kimono as beautiful as a dream spilling on the tiles. I have never seen a human face the color of hers just now, a plummy purplish-red. The baring of her teeth, the puffing of her lips are like a stylized interpretation of grief and rage. She begins to talk, but with such bitter difficulty that it is as though the words are small vital organs being pulled up her throat, phrases like *you said my being a little older and I tried so hard, so hard and you promised that and finally I would do anything,* and at this last her face sprays itself suddenly with falling stars, brilliants, and the big lumber of her body turns toward me and convulses as if about to kneel, I feel the sweat roll down my forehead and Rob says, "Christ, Doreen, what did you expect, a white wedding?" Her vast kimono-clad bulk rears up and goes for him, I throw myself in between and three hundred pounds slams me up against the door, I feel my ribs splintering and her boiling breath in my face, her hands search for my throat as Rob heaves at her polar shoulders, buries his hands in her yellow beehive, and pulls and it lifts away revealing the naked head and jowls of a raving empress, at the same time I cleat rigid fingers to her diamond earbobs and haul like a lunatic and kick out with the steel toes of my boots, she staggers away shrieking, Rob grabs me and wrenches the door open, we pile out, he slams it shut and half-carries, half-drags me to the car, we pile in, he in the driver's seat this time, and as we drive away I hear panels splintering and then shots. Cursing furiously, demon white, Rob slams on the brakes and hauls the car into reverse.

"The old bitch shot at us!" he shouts incredulously. He opens his door and leaps out although I beg him to stop.

"*Stay*," he says, deadly now. Straight as a black arrow he runs into the house. I hear nothing for perhaps ten seconds. Then there are blows too fast to count, one after the other, viciously loud, and a woman crying. My mind flinches away from the thought of his hard fist on the tender pinks and roses of her face. I have trouble connecting these delicate, hopeless sobs— she sounds like an abandoned princess—with the woman I saw. A few seconds later, Rob walks out. He is putting something in his pocket. He climbs into the car, shaking his head and laughing. "Incredible," he says.

I lean my forehead against the car window as Rob drives to the hospital. In the sky, star fields vibrate. Rob speaks just once during the ride. "Repo woman," he says with affection, and pats my knee, and smiles at me.

At the Emergency Room, they listen with astonishment to the lathered knocking of my heart, strap my ribs and send me home. They display impeccable big-city tact and ask nothing about the blood on my gloves, after being assured that it is not mine.

We drive home. He smokes slowly, with a cool serene air, like a young pharaoh. It seems to me that I reek with terror beneath my black clothes. He smells herbal and fresh, a royal babe. I plan my speech to him. I won't be proud or quarrelsome, I will just tell him the truth. *I don't want to die, Rob, I don't want to kill. Please, you must never again—*

Rob turns to say something to me, and sees my face. "No, don't. Don't cry, Rose. Hey, look at me. I'm going to sing like Dion. See how funny I do this." He steadies the steering wheel with his knees, freeing his hands. He begins to sing "The Wanderer" with hammy gestures: "...*where the pretty girls are, well you know that I'm around, / I kiss 'em and I love 'em 'cause to me they're all the same...*" He sings in a tough, world-weary voice, like Dion, with a casual but powerful thump on the steering wheel at the end of each line. "—*and when she asks me which one I love the best / I tear open my shirt I got ROSIE on my chest.*"

He tears open his shirt. Over his heart there is a tattooed rose, with a vine twining around it, and his slim brown hand splays across it triumphantly.

I say nothing, but when we are home he answers me just the same. We are standing in the driveway beside my car, and he's examining a new nick just above the window in the passenger's side. He runs his thumb over it, then turns to go into the house. I make some sad rudimentary sound, a bleat or baa, and he turns back to face me fully. Under the snow sparkle of his blue eyes, I see myself, my poor face with the sweat dried on it.

Rob says, "I want to thank you, Rose. I have a gift for you." Slowly, he reaches into his pocket, and brings something out, grinning. "Close your eyes and open your hand," he says. I close my eyes and hold my black-gloved palm out to him. I feel a tiny weight. When I look, because it's still dark, my irises are confused by a jumble of moonrays in my hand. After a minute, I see they are actually Doreen's two magnificent earrings, richly webbed with diamonds. There are dark stains on the wires, as there were on my gloves.

"Doreen wanted you to have these," Rob says. "Happy now?" He pronounces these words indulgently, as though humoring a difficult child, but I begin to weep. He frowns. He studies my face, looks restlessly away, then back. After a moment he says, "I don't know why you do this to yourself. It's all clear. Someone has to come. Someone has to save me, Mom said so. You're my sister. You promised Mom. And you know that it has to be you. Every time. Every time. Every time."

Usually Rob liked me to cook eggs and bacon when he'd come home again, but this time he went directly to his room. "No," he said coldly. "I don't want any." This was to let me know he was disappointed in me. I heard him collapse on the bed. "I'm so tired," he said. "I'm dead." Within a minute I heard the strange, exhausted respiration of his sleep.

But for me there was no rest. My great fear was that the woman had killed herself. Wasn't that what abandoned princesses in despair did? I stood in the kitchen and fought it out. Finally, I decided I had to go back.

It was palest blue dawn when I stopped across the street from 123 Tudor Lane. I sat in the car, trembling. Suddenly I saw a great bulk, which I could not identify at first, moving in the yard through swirls of mist. A languid flutter of fabric…it was Doreen. She was alive. Slowly my eyes adjusted. She was still wearing the fabulous, blossoming kimono. She swooped low, sleeves curling sumptuously, and I saw the little white shapes winding around her. She was feeding her cats.

I took the diamond earrings from my purse. My ribs stabbed me viciously, and I didn't seem to be breathing, but I climbed out of the car. She straightened and watched me. I crossed the street and walked up to her. I could smell roses and night stocks from her garden, but she was the biggest flower of all, radiating jasmine. I could dimly make out her face. She was bruised, and looked tired and sad, but her eyes belonged to her and not to some crazy woman. She looked more or less all right, even with the new black stitches in her earlobes. I was surprised we hadn't run into each other at the Emergency Room. We gazed at each other, neither of us blinking. I held the earrings out, and after a long minute she took them. Very slowly, we smiled at each other. Then I walked back to the car. The cats danced along behind me as far as the curb.

Now I can rest forever, I thought.

At home, I headed into the bathroom. For the last two months, I'd been hoarding pills. For some reason I paused. I ended up standing in the doorway. Across the hall, I could hear Rob's night breathing. He'd told me many times that he never dreamed. Yet he was an extraordinarily noisy sleeper. He would thrash restlessly, hum pop songs, laugh slyly as though at some rank joke, rap out indecent orders in a hard, hateful voice. Other times, he would utter sweetly coaxing words as though insinuating himself between heart strings. Right now he was purring and yowling in his sleep like a young leopard at the zoo, full of gazelle.

I was not thinking. I was listening. Yet somehow, after several minutes, I crossed to my room and pulled a bag out of the closet. As I packed it, I could still hear him. He laughed quietly to himself as I searched my desk to make sure I wasn't leaving checks or credit cards behind. He scolded and mocked as the door closed behind me. An impossibly long, incandescent snore pursued me through his window as I walked to the car.

I tried to leave the city. I backtracked, made U-turns, plunged down new routes, rejected them. For an hour, I drove gigantic circles around the house where I'd spent my whole life.

I didn't know where I should go. I didn't know where I would be, or how it would turn out. Finally, I realized it didn't matter. I would be where he was not. Every one of these highways was paved in pure gold.

I took the nearest exit and drove like hell.

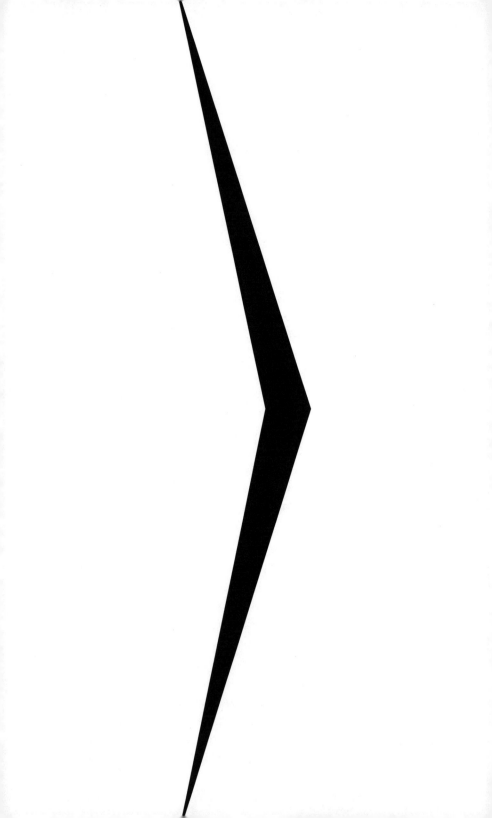

JAMES PORTER HUNTS MUSHROOMS

"Because I'm afraid of what I might do," James said quietly. "Because I'm afraid I could murder her."

Father Karl was silent with astonishment. He'd been listening to James Porter's confessions for twenty years. Last Saturday, the man had confessed as sins his pride in a certain mauve silk shirt and eating a few grapes at the market without paying for them. This was very typical of James. And his wife Laura was, if possible, even more devout. Dead center on her bosom, she always wore a gold crucifix blessed by the Pope. But today, James was saying he could cut her throat. Father Karl felt as though a quiet tributary had suddenly burst its banks and was plunging straight toward him, swollen with uprooted trees and destroyed houses and sexy female carcasses as dead as Eve.

When James finally stopped, Father Karl was silent. For the first time in his career in the priesthood, he had no idea at all what penance to suggest. He turned his face away so that James would not see the horror in it, and his eyes fell on James's mushroom kit.

Earlier that day, James had gone home to pack some gear in his car. He'd gotten the afternoon off so that he could pursue his hobby, hunting and picking wild mushrooms. James the great morel-stalker. People had laughed about it for years. What other man from the neighborhood ever left the big, boiling city to drive on purpose into the country, braving all the little wild animals, their teeth and claws and filthy diseases, the godforsaken hazards and messes of nature? Why stumble around in the underbrush getting torn by thorns, stepping in shit, and at the end of a long sweaty day, return with ruined clothes, all ecstatic over a palmful of dubious fungus? Laura was such a good wife that she did add these brown little nubbins to omelettes. But everyone agreed James's pride in the smelly morsels was comic. And as for his look of tranquillity and peace when he came home from these country days—well, quiet James had always been a little different.

He opened the hall door. The good home smells—cooking, beeswax polish, rose, vanilla—met him. He was just about to walk into the kitchen when he heard a man's voice, one he'd hoped never to hear again. The man was the owner, a brutally demanding one, of a tire factory where James had worked years before. James stood still in astonishment. Then he cautiously moved a few feet to the left so that he could see into the kitchen.

Laura and Brett Turner stood face to face. James barely recognized his wife. She was a slim, angelically pale blonde, and usually she looked something like a human Easter lily. But today she was a burning rose, furious, aroused, and wildly alive. The man and woman were not touching, but their posture of rage was more intimate than an embrace.

"Who do you think you are?" the man said now to Laura in a quiet voice more chilling than a shout. "Ruling your world, issuing your proclamations. Why do you stay with him? Because he's the only man on your block who wears a tie to work? Although personally, I think it's stretching it to wear a tie to sort mail. Or maybe you think your priest will be mad at you if you divorce him?"

He lifted the gold cross at her breast, attached to its rich chain. He said, "Has your life been so easy, are you so cold, that only false things make you feel?" He regarded the cross in his palm. He said, as though innocently seeking to know, "Why do you wear this? Have you forgotten the things we've done while this was around your neck?" Suddenly he leaned close and whispered viciously in her ear. She began to weep. He looked at Laura, full into her exquisite agonized face, and very slowly his own face changed. His hand rose, and with dreamlike gentleness, his fingers followed the course of tears down her cheek. She turned her head and kissed his hand.

Once James had been driving home through the country at night, happy in his way under the moonless sky. The darkness felt secure. He turned a corner and suddenly faced an inferno, a house ablaze from attic to cellar, nailed up against the black night like a meteor. A crowd of little people rushed here and there, wringing their hands, throwing buckets of water, crying and praying. But the great fireball that had been a home consumed itself, and the night sky cared nothing for their anguish.

He looked around the hall, trembling. He saw his mushroom kit by the door. Silently, he took it and left. When he was standing on the sidewalk, he realized that he did not know where to go. After a minute, he began walking toward the church.

The sun was still high overhead. James had hiked for an hour and now he had reached it, the secret valley he'd discovered the year before. He'd spotted it as a perfect habitat for morels, kept his eye on the place with a gloating, almost sensuous zeal, and waited for spring. Now it was May.

Father Karl had commanded him, just for today, to think of nothing except this valley. "Not Laura. Not the man. I forbid you to think of hatred, and cutting. Just concentrate on the day and the mushrooms. An ordinary day in the woods. Give God some time. He will tell you what to do."

For his first hour in the wood, James could think of nothing except hatred and cutting. He thought: *Father Karl is a priest. He does not understand.* His heart hurt so badly that, at first, he wished he was dead. But gradually, habit took over. He began to notice the perfect habitat. There were morels here. He could smell them as a dog smells truffles.

He moved into the cooler darkness of pine trees, many of them dead. When he reached a stand of old elms that had a strangely seared appearance, he paused, then walked around and beyond them.

He stood in a natural amphitheater of elms and poplars, all of which had been scorched by fire the year before. The trees lived, but damage had been done. The burn had been contained in this remote area; and the only way he could explain it was that the fire must have started from a lightning strike, and been drowned in a few minutes by heavy rain.

There was a dark, pungent smell, with the earth in it, and soaked mosses. Some might have called it a reek; to him it was a vital perfume. It came with the treasure.

Morels were everywhere. There were tiny golden sponge-capped ones no bigger than a finger, others of a meaty dark brown like a hulking man's fist. The fingerlings popped up through pine needles and leaves, sheltered beneath May flowers or butted their honeycomb heads against grey bark. The big ones shouldered up out of the sod any which way they could, snaking through roots, muscling rocks, sometimes with blossoms and animal scat on their heads. Large and small, they were stone determined to emerge, powered by their eerie unstoppable growth.

James began to fill his baskets, almost breathlessly. But, when he paused, some tiny humps in leaf litter caught his eye. He hesitated, then brushed the leaves aside. The bright-yellow horns of chanterelles rose, curly-edged. James sat back on his heels in surprise. Chanterelles did not grow before midsummer.

James stared at the scorched elms and beeches surrounding him, then back at the chanterelles. Perhaps this new habitat, purified by fire, speeded growth. He picked one and smelled it. The delicate apricot fragrance penetrated all the way to the back of his skull. He nibbled it, and the scent became the taste. He picked several, eagerly, adding them to his basket. But no sooner had he done that, than his eye fell on an enormous bracket fungus, at least two feet across, growing on an elm. A Dryad's Saddle? He had never seen one. And that tuft of orange-capped, dark-stemmed mushrooms with pale yellow gills, growing on a decaying stump? Surely that was a Velvet Foot. Yet he knew Velvet Foot grew only in the East.

Thoroughly puzzled, James stood up and looked about him with sweeping superstitious glances. He knew that, after a burn, the woods exploded with fruiting bodies. That was to be expected. But, from so far away…? His head bent, he carefully considered the tiny fungus in his hand, two thousand miles from its proper home. Then, very slowly, he began to smile. Well, whether the Velvet Foot spores were borne here on angels' wings or bird shit, they were a gift. And he would accept.

In the next hour, he found at least a dozen genuses whose existence here he would have called impossible.

At length, he reached a sandy area of the clearing. It was completely bare except for a single small cactus. James told himself that, with all he had seen in the last hour, he should not be surprised to have this mescal rear up at his foot. So many of the men he knew would have given a lot to find that plant. They would have snatched at the buds, crammed them down their throats careless of thorns, and rocked like dogs all night. But it was James Porter, who went to Mass every day, who found the mescal. He had to laugh.

James brought his face close to the floral discs and studied them with close attention. Then he lightly touched the dark, dried peyote buds. Curious, he picked several. Their intricate, tightly folded shapes looked like bizarre adornments in his palm. It was at this moment that James first saw the cat.

The animal was standing in the shadows at the foot of a dead pine, watching him. Feral cats sometimes grow very large, and so James was not startled by its size. It had a big-muscled body and a rich coat of dark, burnished gold. Even in shadow, he could see the piercing gem-blue gaze. It was altogether as beautiful a living object as he had ever seen. Yet there was some oddity in its appearance, barely glimpsed in the shadows, that made him uneasy. Cautiously, he walked toward the cat until he could see it clearly.

The animal had a great red burn in its side. This had only half-healed to an angry shield-shaped scar. All around the scar waved the shining fronds of its thick golden coat. James looked into the cat's blue eyes, then at its burn, stared out into the sunny fields and woods, then back at the eyes. The animal stood patiently, bearing its wound, its beauty, and its terrible loneliness.

After a minute James said aloud, "Yes, that's it. That is the way things are."

He did not plan to do it, but his hand moved to his mouth, and his teeth seized the peyote buds. He chewed, chewed. Once he looked up and said to the cat, laughing, "Sorry I'm not saving any for you—" but then the mescaline hit the back of his head like a bomb. There was a great, rushing bloom of darkness before his eyes, then one of light. He fell to the ground, trembling violently.

He could not be sure if it was he who trembled, or if it was the earth which shook against him hatefully, trying to buck him loose. He clung to the ground in terror, extended his arms and legs to hold as much of it down as possible. He felt the individual grains of sand beneath his lathering heart. He turned over and saw himself from above, a man starfish swimming in the desert. He was not at all surprised to note other sealife, exquisitely colored, swimming back and forth before his eyes, even a golden carp, which slowly grew to the size of a galleon. Its languidly swirling tail swept stars and moons in its wake. James stared, then laughed in joy at the radiant strangeness of the vision. The carp's noble and dignified progress against the night sky—but when had it become night?—was something like a comet's swoop, infinitely slowed.

James wanted to share this vision with someone, but there was only the cat. He looked around and was startled to see the animal almost on top of him, right at his shoulder. But James found that he had been mistaken, because it was a cougar, not a cat, whose hot, bloody breath was fanning his face. Also, his coat had darkened—now it seemed black in patches—and the scar in his side burned red as though there were embers in it.

"That fish is too big, even for you," James said, speaking his thoughts aloud, pointing to the carp. Now the carp had turned to an immense golden dirigible, ringed with bands of light, and it was floating away.

"That is what you think," the cougar said.

James was surprised to find that the cougar could talk. However, he did not want to seem ignorant or unworldly, so he concealed his surprise. "Oh," he said sarcastically, "so you're king over the fish? Including whales?"

"Yes," the cougar said. "I am the lord of all."

James looked up, and the word SACRILEGE seemed to write itself very slowly, in huge red letters, each as big as an elephant leg, across the black sky. James jumped up, afraid, and walked away from the beast. *God will be mad at me*, he thought, *if I stay around this cougar.*

For some time, a mad restlessness had been growing in James. He felt it as a surge of strength in his arms and legs, as though his back were broader, his shoulders hungry for any burden. Suddenly he bent against a sapling and fastened his hands around the trunk. He could feel every striation in the bark. He pulled, pulled, and slowly the tree rose from the ground. His heart hammered with joy. He pulled up a few more trees, just to make sure he could do it. He put his hand over his heart to feel its beat, then looked down in surprise. His smooth chest, tense with muscles, rose and fell so calmly. It came to him: *I wish Laura could see me.* This thought kept returning, so powerfully, and with such a burden of yearning, that suddenly he had to steel himself against weeping.

He held his head, that bursting ball, in his hands and plunged wildly around the clearing ten times, twenty times, to stop thought. He made a dead run toward a copse of thorn trees and forced his way through them like a crazy buffalo. He felt the thorn wounds as the claws of hags, infuriating him and yet making his body burn with a mania of strength. He flung himself on his stomach and bucked and forked his body from one edge of the clearing to the other, twisting and screaming aloud as he had seen rodeo broncos do, to throw off a cruel rider.

He was aware the whole time that the cougar watched him. The cougar had continued to grow. His splendid coat was now entirely dark. The red embers in his wound blazed. It came to James that, if he had not been a good Catholic, he would have considered this magnificent beast a proper object of worship.

"James?" the cougar said. Something in James moved strangely at the sound of his name in the cougar's mouth.

"James," the cougar said, "I have watched you all this night and admired the man you have become. Look at yourself."

James looked down his body, along his arms. His clothes were bloody, and hung from him in shreds. Yet his pride grew as he looked at himself. It was as though he saw his body clearly for the first time. It was corded all over with muscles like a hero's. His hair, which had always been arranged in a neat ponytail according to Laura's preferences, now curled densely over his head and shoulders. His limbs were like young trees. He felt that at will he could leap over this forest, run the forty miles home and show—show her—but he refused to form this thought.

"I know," the cougar said quietly, as though his big paw had laid open James's brain and he could follow his thought tracks. "You could show her what you have become. You could love her so strong she would never think of anyone else." James looked away. He was afraid to listen; afraid to hope. "But you are here now," the cougar contiued in a stronger voice, "and you need to prove to me that you are worthy of a new life." James was silent, absorbing this thought. The cougar said, "You know that I am a mighty lord. I have dominion even over the angels. At my will, they increase or decrease. At my will, I send them swaggering over the heavens—" and he gestured with his chin at the wing-shaped starfield of the Milky Way in the night sky, "—or make them sit like little white tulips in this hand." Gravely he held his ebony paw out to James, the black pads up. James flinched away from the steel claws so close, each of them as long as his face, and the cougar smoothly retracted them.

"You must absorb one of these angels," the cougar said matter-of-factly. "You must get its divinity inside yourself. I'll show you how. Follow me." Without waiting for James's response, the cougar turned like a dancer on its paws and headed straight into the forest. Mighty trees bowed outward as the animal walked between them, his black fur stroking the dark.

They reached a clearing deep in the forest. The racing stars swarmed above the bit of earth on which they stood. The cougar breathed in deeply, locating a spoor, then with nose and paw began shifting underbrush. Delicately, he moved mounds of acrid leaves aside, and finally revealed them: dozens of shining white mushrooms, tender and delicate in form. Lacy volvas swathed their throats, the slender stalks stood on a single basal foot, and were topped by broad white hats.

"My holy girls," the cougar said fondly. "My little angels."

James knelt and stared. He said, "But those are Destroying Angels."

"Nonsense," the cougar said dismissively. "I bewitched them just for you. You must eat, embrace their divinity. Your body will shine like a star, your heart, belly, entrails, everything. Your whole life will become a track of light."

James looked at the cougar steadily, for such a long moment that the animal's eyes fell. Then he looked at the little angels. Their glowing white sides reminded him of something.

"Yes, I know," the cougar said, hearing his thought. "They are like your wife's skin."

James reached down and picked them, seven, eight, nine, ten, filling both hands.

"You won't need so many," the cougar said.

James admired their beauty in his palms, but was careful not to hold them too close. He knew that even their scent was toxic.

The cougar said, "I'm told they taste good. Eat, James."

Slowly, James looked up at the cougar. "But who could have told you how they taste?" he said. "Dead people are silent."

The cougar blinked. He looked down as though collecting himself. When he finally looked up, James felt impaled on the ice-blue knives of his eyes. Yet when the cougar spoke, his voice was sweetly reasonable.

"You see, James," he said, "somebody has to die. Either you or Laura. You could hide a few of these little white ladies in your basket, and the first bite Laura eats would be her last. Or you could sacrifice yourself, as your noble nature demands. But somebody has to die."

James stared back down at his own hands filled with the luminous white forms. Then in the next instant, he did not know how it happened, but one of his strong brown hands sprang up and crammed a fistful of mushrooms into the beast's nostrils. "Smell," James said. As the cougar gasped for air his huge jaws gaped open, and now the man saw his other hand push a second fistful of mushrooms deep in this maw, past razor teeth and plush, bloody tongue, ramming the poison angels where they belonged with the full strength of his arm.

"Eat," James said, and backed away fast.

The cougar's whole vast body trembled. He looked at James blindly, the flower-blue irises now all ebony pupil. The conflagration in his side lit up the whole forest as he fell to his knees, and then crashed down, bucking and thrashing. A sound began to come, the respiration of a death agony, but it did not seem to come from one throat. Every wild being under the sky convulsed in that strangling rasp of breath.

Finally, all was quiet again. James turned around, and the animal lay dead in a bloom of light. His whole body shone like a star, every artery a jeweled track. James put his hand to the beast's side. He could feel the mighty ribs like the arch of rocks that uphold the earth, but no heartbeat. *Well, he said somebody had to die,* James thought, and in spite of everything, he smiled a little. He moved his hand to the site of the burning wound, yet he felt no heat or blood. In fact, on the cougar's whole shining black flank, and in the silver veins underneath, there was no sign of a wound at all.

))))

"Why won't that crazy old fool give it up?" Jon said in a low voice to Ray. Then he felt funny because he'd called a priest a fool. But Ray had told and told the old guy that there was nothing more they could do, they had to organize a search party. Even Father Karl should listen to a sheriff. But nothing would stop him, they could hear him this minute plunging through the woods right where there were all those thorn trees, and he was still shouting with his destroyed voice for James Porter. And he had been like this for three hours. At first, goaded by his manic energy, Jon and the sheriff had forced their way through the underbrush too, and up and down ravines and through streams, until they were more dead than alive. But now they sat exhausted in the truck, listening to the priest's shouts.

Everything about the clearing gave the sheriff the creeps. The maimed trees were bad enough, and that mescal which looked as though it had been eaten alive. But it was the naked hand-prints and footprints in the sand which shocked him. They covered every inch of the clearing, lapping and overlapping many times. Even on the surrounding trees, there were bloody prints extending up as far as a man could reach.

"There must have been a lot of people here," Jon said in a hushed voice. "The poor son of a bitch was murdered in some kind of gang initiation, maybe."

"No," Ray said. "There was just the one man. The prints are all from the same person. I don't think he was murdered. There's no trail of blood, no corpse. " He too spoke quietly, as though the priest could hear them.

"Then what—"

"How the fuck do I know?" Wearily, Ray opened the door of the truck and climbed out. He looked again at the thousands of impressions in the sand, the same hands and feet going every-where, going nowhere. He looked at the bloody handprints scrab-bling up the tree trunks. Trying to get out, he thought. "Those buds can make a man pretty crazy. If he's dead somewhere, he died of—" he hesitated, then snapped sarcastically, "he danced too hard, okay?"

"He boogied right out of his clothes?" Jon held up the plastic evidence bag, which contained a torn khaki shirt and shorts.

"Maybe the man enjoys running around in his underpants," Ray said coldly. "He's not the first, and he won't be the last."

For several minutes they were silent, listening to the priest's yells. Now he sounded much further away.

"I don't know how somebody so old and so fat can keep go-ing on like that," Jon said.

"James Porter owes him a lot, if he's still alive. His wife didn't know where he was."

When they'd first arrived, they expected to find Porter may-be drunk and passed out beside a campfire, or howling and help-less with a broken leg. But he was not here, not anywhere they searched. It was then that the priest became frantic.

Ray had taken numerous pictures of the clearing, and then the forest, because it had to be done. He almost successfully con-cealed the deathly loathing which overcame him among these dank trees. He took pictures of the shattered trunks and boughs.

In everything Ray did, he felt himself watched, and not by Jon or the priest. He forced himself to complete every task, to neglect nothing, but it was with the cruelest effort of his life. And now he and Jon sat in the truck, sweating with fear in the freez-ing dawn, waiting for the priest to give it up.

At last, Father Karl stumbled from the woods and slowly approached the truck. Ray and Jon tried not to stare, but the priest looked worse than any insane or homeless person they had ever seen. His black clothes were ripped and filthy, and his face bloodied in a dozen places. Father Karl saw their eyes. He looked down at his coat, then touched his face and stared at his torn hands. Finally he looked up and said simply, "I'm his priest. I baptized him. I gave him his First Communion, and I married him to Laura."

They left. Jon drove, and he hit the ruts so hard they felt it in their skeletons. It seemed they couldn't get away fast enough. The truck screamed over the gullies and up hills. Jon was taking the chances of a fool with this terrain, but neither Ray nor the priest corrected him. Because even when they had reached the road, even when they were many miles from the clearing, it was as though they were flayed by a gaze. And this gaze did not just see them. It smothered their heads like a caul. It branded their necks with burning letters they could not interpret. It speared straight through them, with grimness and joy.

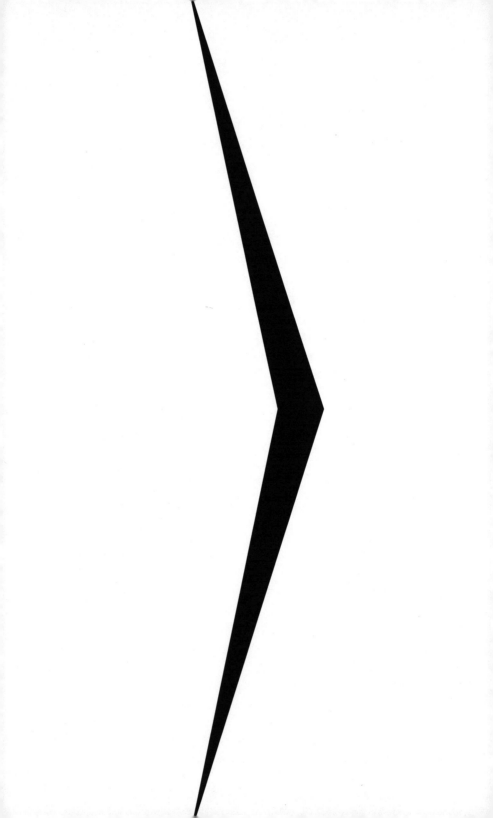

MARRYING JERRY

I met Jerry at a time when I knew damn well I didn't have a life. This happens periodically to people who read a lot. I met him at his health food store. The store was a little marvel of color and order. I would drag myself there on the days when I felt parched and weazened, when life had been a bitch. I would waveringly negotiate the step on the threshold, even the hem of my tragic winter coat drooping with multiple deficiencies. The instant I was inside, I was aware of the compact, humming heart of the store. Every worker knew what to do. Fruits were sold only in their season, and faithful customers like me understood why it would be wrong to carry strawberries home over ice and snow. We felt the sun-strength emanating from the little round yolks of the fertilized eggs.

Jerry was scrubbed and sexy, in a working-stiff, populist kind of way. We became friends over the unfiltered honey vat when nobody else was in the store. The vat was glass, and he noticed a little brown thing in the bottom, under the gummy honey-sea. Big Jerry stripped his shirt off, scrubbed his arm like a surgeon, said "Don't take pictures, they'd close me down," and plunged his arm up to the pit into the vat. His fingers closed on the brown object at the bottom and he brought it up, his other hand stripping honey from his arm as it hit the air. He squinted at the twig-like thing. "It's all right," he said. "It's a flower stem." I stared at the bronze animal hairs on his arm, all glazed and matted with gold. My tongue clove to the roof of my mouth, witless with lust. I actually wondered if he would take it amiss if I offered to lick the honey off his arm.

I did no such thing, of course. We became better friends, gradually. He rototilled my garden without being asked, brought flowers unexpectedly, and later on, cooked me big range break-fasts. He was also as good as he could be, attending study groups at the local Unitarian church. This was a special church where you did not have to believe in God and Jesus, but instead, learned how to tread lightly on the earth. He studied parenting methods of wolf packs, handed out MEAT IS DEAD stickers at his store, and shared advice about how to treat your partner lovingly and caringly, and without wasteful expenditure.

Jerry used to hand me out of his old pickup truck like a rich jewel.

One time I said something, very hesitatingly, about my plain face. "It doesn't matter," he said, so simply that I knew he meant it. "Besides," he continued, "you have such a beautiful body!"

And so we were married. Jerry wrote the ceremony, in which we loudly, and repeatedly, stated the immaculateness of our intent toward each other.

Our life continued quietly. I quit my job and began working at Jerry's store. Evenings we would walk home, hand in hand, and for supper Jerry would make me magnificent sandwiches. I ate his Denver sandwiches with butter running down my arm. I could hardly chew, because of the big smile I had on my face in those days.

After about six months, Jerry decided that he believed in God and Jesus after all, and joined a new church. The members in this church referred to the Bible as the Big Book, a term which formerly I'd associated with the AA manual.

My lack of faith bothered Jerry. When his birthday rolled around he asked me, sweetly and lovingly, to read Genesis aloud to him as his gift. So I did. Then he asked me to read him Exodus for Christmas, Leviticus for Valentine's Day, and so forth. I realized that he intended to coax me by baby steps through the entire Bible. My private reaction was that many of these Old Testament holy men were as big a collection of bullying, lying, fornicating rogues and felons as I'd always suspected. However, I bit my lip. It seemed to me that, if my love for Jerry was true,

I should be willing to read him the Bible word by word to give him pleasure.

Around the time I reached Numbers, Jerry came home from Bible study all excited. A new star was now heading the church, a famous evangelist whose name was Sister Lorna. Sister Lorna had recently published a book, *Let the Angels Call the Shots*. Her theory was that each of us has an angel twin, invisible but with dazzling powers. Our task is to learn to plug into this personal angel. Our twin, having access to the wisdom of the ages, can tell us what to do so we'll never be at a loss. We just have to learn how to keep the passage between their mouth and our ear lubricated and clear.

Lorna had also given the study group some bold new information about the old days, when the Big Book was being written. She said that the men who wrote the Ten Commandments, including the seventh, "Thou shalt not commit adultery," were all polygamists. Jerry seemed very struck by this. In retrospect, it seems an ominous piece of information to stick in a husband's mind.

Jerry invited Sister Lorna to dinner. She arrived on a plum-soft June evening, in a huge white Cadillac with a zebra-striped interior. She was a large woman and wore a big white suit, with various tactful drapes over her whopping bosoms and big butt. She had a sticker on her car that said, MEAT WEEPS. *Oh, shit,* I thought, remembering the crown roast in the oven. It smelled rendingly delicious.

"How is your name spelled?" she asked me, when Jerry introduced us.

"B-e-l-l-e."

"May I call you Bella? B-e-l-l-e always makes me think of Belly." And Lorna laughed ripplingly.

"Well, L-o-r-n-a always makes me think of *frigging moron*," I said, but only to myself.

Jerry was wearing some broad purple suspenders I'd never seen before. He was scrubbed so clean that his ruddy cheeks shone. When we sat down at the table, he carved the roast. He looked doubtful and apologetic as he offered it to her. "Do you eat meat? Will you have—"

"A slice of corpse? I think not," she said, and laughed merrily again. But in the end she ate a lot of the roast.

We drank a lot that evening. A pungent aroma of smoke and blood filled the kitchen. The roast had been rare, the kind that makes you remember that carne, meat, is the root of carnal. Lorna's beestung lips (collagened, I thought) gleamed fatly with oils and wine. At some point, very late in the evening, I noticed how silent Jerry had become. He watched as Lorna wrapped those lips around seared suet, hunks of Roma tomatoes, the blue veins of soft-reeking cheeses. She noisily sucked and nibbled her way through meaty bones, bulbs of green onions, bittersweet chocolate leaves on the Queen of Sheba cake. I have to admit, that woman knew how to enjoy a meal. She put her whole back into it.

Jerry watched her. It had become very dark in the room, and I was thinking how I should turn on the overhead light when Jerry suddenly got up and went to the counter. He put several small votive candles on a tray and lit them. In the darkness, he brought the candles to the table and set them before Lorna like an offering of flowers. I was confused at being left in the dark, and by the dazzle of their two bright heads above the flares of light.

After that, Lorna would often swoop by on especially beautiful summer evenings. She would accept iced tea, converse. Immaculately clad in a white sundress with a sweetheart neckline, she made the wicker lawn chairs creak. Once she laughed so hard at Jerry's jokes that her nose bled. I think it was that evening that she bethought herself of some church business that needed Jerry's immediate attention, and she bore him off in her white Caddy.

As she cropped up night after night, her wild Nordic head flaring in the red dusk, I came to think of her as a Viking raider.

It seemed to me that those big, terrifyingly direct turquoise eyes were fixed on my one treasure. But Jerry said Lorna only cared about God and Jesus, and was obsessed with interpreting their will through her angel twin.

Five years before—hell, a year before—I would have laughed at the idea of loving a man who could make a statement like that. But not now.

What is it for: this fierce particularity of yearning, which makes incandescent one human object, and no other?

Jerry had always had a wonderfully hot, carnal attentiveness. Now he grew cool. He was increasingly silent and distracted, and in the twilight, would look down the street in the direction Lorna might come. He watched the street like a dog.

It was during this period that I found a press-on nail stuck to his underwear.

I said nothing to Jerry about this. Instead, I spent a great deal of time driving around in my car with the radio on. Country songs, the kind I'd always made fun of, spoke directly to my condition. *I know he doesn't treat you right. I see the tears you try to hide.* I changed the station and got Buddy Holly singing "Slippin' and Slidin'." *I won't be your fool no more.* Some hope. I rotated the dial. It was starting to rain hard, and just then Bessie Smith wailed suddenly, Oh it was honey this and honey that and it was love sweet love all the time. She also sang a song about a woman who murdered her husband. He wallowed around and then he died. It seemed to me that this was a good representation of the human condition in general. You wallowed around, and then you died.

I thought a bookstore might cheer me up. The big Borders was open. As it turned out, there was a huge pyramid of Lorna's bestseller, *Let the Angels Call the Shots*, in the front window. I picked up a copy and looked at it. I was interested in the mental make-up of someone who thought the angels told her to ball my husband. *Thou shalt ball Jerry.* Truly God must be everywhere. I looked at the chapter headings. The one called "Love Yourself Tender" caught my eye. I turned to it. Lorna was a big believer in self-love, being crazy about yourself. You deserved, she explained, the absolute best of everything, and should always think of yourself as the guest of honor at life's banquet. I thought of Jerry buck naked on a huge silver trencher at the table, an apple in his mouth. Lorna said that to signify her complete self-love and self-acceptance, she began every day by giving herself a great big hug. Everyone else should do the same.

I put the book down. Tentatively, I encircled myself with my arms. Was I doing it right? I felt thin. My heart beat gravely beneath my wrist. After a minute, in a movement that felt irrepressible, my shoulders hunched, my chin drew down to my chest. I closed my eyes. I stood there for quite some time before realizing that people, a lot of them, were staring at me. A man said in an interested voice, "That's the first time I ever saw anybody sleep in the fetal position standing up."

I drove around for a long time, then bought a bottle and drove to the store. I let myself in. I got drunk. In fact, I hadn't been this drunk since college, when one night I mistook my roommate's bureau drawer for the bathroom.

My memories of that night in the store are hazy, but I clearly remember a moment toward dawn when I stood in front of the glass honey vat, with my face over it. I was attempting to weep exactly three tears into the vat: not two, and not four, but three, which for some reason I thought was the appropriate number as laid down by fairy tales.

I'll speed this up. When I drove home that morning, I discovered Jerry and Sister Lorna in the shower together. They didn't notice me at first. I looked at them coldly. They were both big, pink people. In fact, I was kind of amazed to see how big the two of them were. It was like watching Moby Dick and his mate prance and thrash, gone to blubber but still capable of some high-wailing whale music. I reached in and turned off the cold water. This was followed by their tornado-siren shrieks.

I've heard of adrenaline rushes, but still can't understand how I walked into our bedroom, hauled the big mattress off the bed and down two flights of stairs, and burned it in the front yard. It was a California King, and I'm barely five feet tall. It was interesting to see how quickly the police showed up. We'd been robbed the month before, and that time it took them much longer.

The profoundly shaken, scalded Jerry demanded a divorce. At the hearing, the judge left us alone for fifteen minutes to see if we could reconcile. The reconciliation got off on the wrong foot. Jerry mentioned at once Lorna's belief that, once in every generation, there is a reincarnation of the Great Beast of Revelations. She thought I might be it. I responded that Lorna was a moronic slut, and if she didn't keep her fat ass out of my life, I would drink her blood like wine. Jerry looked horrified, and yet oddly satisfied. Apparently, I had spoken exactly as a Great Beast should.

The remaining fourteen minutes and forty five seconds we sat in silence. At the last possible instant, as Jerry got up, he looked at me and said, "You may not believe it, but I'm sorry for you. I'm sorry you have nothing and no one." Then he walked out of the room.

It was true that I had no one. Not a person in the world cared if I lived or died.

But Jerry was wrong when he said I had nothing. A conference with lawyers had been scheduled. Six hours into it, when everyone had said his piece not once but many times, when Jerry shouted until blood vessels burst in his eyes and he made as if to throw a leather armchair at me and his lawyer had to clinch him in a bear hug to stop him, when they'd finally left, my lawyer looked at me with exhaustion, but a sort of fugitive respect, and said, "Congratulations. You got your prairie justice. You do have that. And I bet it tastes pretty damn good."

When the sun was setting and I walked down the courthouse steps, it is true I was alone. But I owned the store.

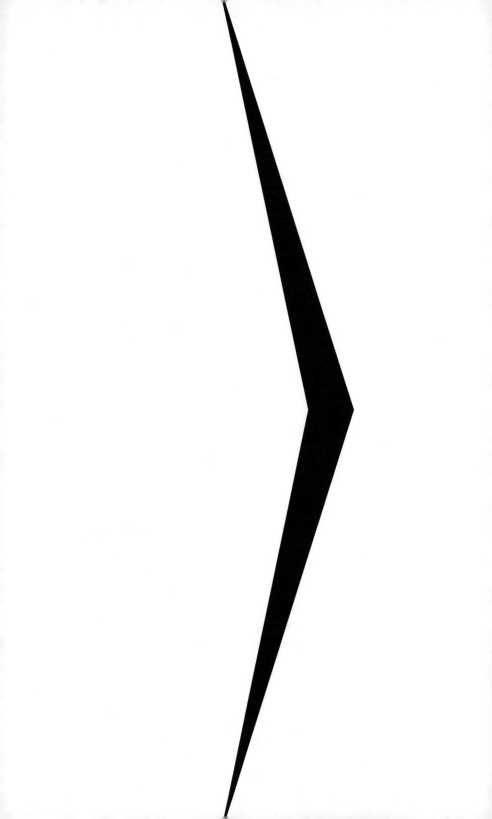

MAERA'S DAY

"He's doing it again," Amy whispered with shocked delight. Siobhan Reilly, who was arranging the romaine display, paused with her hands in crushed ice. She turned, unsmiling, to watch Juan Maera as he caressed the fruit in her shop.

He slowly, sensuously pressed his thumb into the soft parts of a cantaloupe. He weighed little melons in his hands, and tweaked their tips. He palmed bananas, considered their length, and smiled smugly. With the tip of a finger, he lewdly bobbled sugar grapes. Siobhan flushed with outrage.

"Did you talk to the lawyer about it?" Amy whispered.

"Yes," Siobhan said. "He says there is no law against groping fruit. He says that if Maera made some sound, moaned or sighed, maybe we could get him on a charge of public indecency—"

"No," Amy said sadly. "He is silent." She watched Maera twiddle kiwis, his eyes closed ecstatically. Bursting with curiosity, she hissed to Siobhan, "If he's so rich, why does he wear those old clothes? And why does he act this way?"

Siobhan said, "Mr. Maera has always enjoyed driving me crazy, from the time we were children. He thinks I'm a prude. Also, his reasoning powers are shot because he has struggled all his life with religious doubts. He is an atheist."

Siobhan, who was the president of St. Rita's Altar Society, said this in exactly the same tone she would have used to say Maera had a cleft hoof. Many years before, they had both been students at St. Rita's Parochial School. Her teacher, Sister Ursula, described an atheist as a naked, pitiful figure of stick and bone, nailed to blasted rock and suffering alone under steely skies. Saints disguised as hawks would ferociously swoop down to sport with him. Oh, they would know what to do with his splinty limbs and the poor addled grill of his brains. Siobhan shuddered.

"You know," Amy said, her eye following Maera, "if it weren't for those terrible clothes, and his limp, he would be very handsome." She spoke with the sumptuous confidence of the beautiful.

The two women worked together in silence for several minutes, arranging the melon and apple displays. Finally Siobhan said, "I lived across the street from him when we were children. I knew his mother and father. When you consider everything— that is, when you take into account—" she stopped, then shook her head. And in spite of Amy's questions, she would not say another word.

When Maera approached the counter, Siobhan promised herself, as she always did, that she would not give him the satisfaction of scolding him for his unmentionable behavior in her store. It just made him worse. But as he stood at the counter, courteously placing the cantaloupe he had goosed close to the scales for her convenience, and making innocent remarks about the plump lusciousness of the peaches, as always her outrage burst forth.

"Juan," she said icily, "I must, once again, demand that you confine your excesses to your private life."

"Oh, Siobhan, why grudge me a little fun? And just what is this private life you refer to? What excesses?" He raised his hands, those tricky hands now glistening with plum juice, palms up. "I have no time for them. I am a slave to my business. Two hundred newsstands. Sixty, eighty, a hundred hours a week—" His head turned like a sunflower as buxom Amy walked past the window, light beams bouncing off her yellow froth of curls. She gleamed with gel and solar power, like an exotic generator. His eyes narrowed, and he followed her progress down the aisle with an abominable smile. He did this every day, and every day Siobhan's hand itched to slap him silly.

Their ritual complete, he next went to Miller's Jewelers. The diamond lay in the jeweler's palm like a hard little earth shimmering with blue flame. "The finest blue diamond I have ever offered," he said. His offhand tone indicated that he was so sure of his ground there was no need for bombast. He was only slightly discomfited when Juan Maera whipped a jeweler's glass out of his frayed shirt pocket. It was well known that Maera, for all his wealth, was a fanatic about getting his money's worth. Nobody could make the eagle scream like Juan.

He put the glass in his eye, bent toward the diamond, and regarded it with such intense concentration that the jeweler felt uneasily he was calling the blue soul of the stone into his own keeping without benefit of cash exchange. Maera's horrible father had been a grifter and a wife-beater, after all. A good looking man and a sharp dresser, but a monster. Blood would tell.

"Turn it over," Juan said.

Miller obliged, smiling agreeably, flipping the jewel to reveal its underside. He thought to himself, *Just like the suspicious little bastard to think I'm selling him one with a rotten spot, like it was a cantaloupe. Although I would if I could.*

"Wrap it up," Juan said.

As Miller brought out a little velvet box, he dared to smile significantly and say, "A superb jewel of carbon to adorn a jewel of flesh."

Juan stared at him in icy wonder, silently, as though the jeweler had committed some bestial vulgarity so stupefying that words failed him. Without taking his eyes away, he felt his various ragged pockets. Eventually he brought out a greasy wad of bills. When Miller saw the denominations he felt light-headed, as though the bills had been injected directly into a major vein.

When Juan had left, Miller told his assistant, "Whoever she is, she must be something."

People had been gossiping about Juan's mysterious mistress for years. He, who lived so humbly and ascetically in spite of his wealth, evidently believed only the very best was good enough for her. She lived in glamorous seclusion, nobody knew exactly where. The nightdresses he bought for her, so modestly cut they could have been worn by a convent schoolgirl, were embroidered by Spanish nuns and frilled with antique lace.

He was regarded with deep suspicion by the salesgirls when he bought these night-dresses. The rich men they knew staggered through the lingerie department like jovial bulls foraging for wine-fed heifers, arms full of satin jungle prints, garters comically dangling their fuchsia rosettes, bustiers in glinting limes and acid pinks flung pell-mell over no-nonsense biceps.

Juan even selected her fruit himself, peach by peach, looking for sweet healthfulness in their round cheeks. He, who wouldn't buy himself a decent shirt, commissioned artisans to make furniture of rare woods, lovingly scaled to her petite stature.

"He is a man in love," the merchants told each other. "And whoever she is, she is short, and she is beautiful."

After Juan bought the blue diamond, he went to Santo's Meat Market. This was his favorite stop. He noted with satisfaction that there were no other customers. A year before, Santo's estranged wife Linda had had her husband charged with domestic abuse. Juan, who was an old school friend of Linda's, paid her legal bills. "Juan Maera is one tough cookie," Linda's mother said at the time, "but he has a little piece of sugar in him."

Santo escaped jail time. "After all, it is impossible to abuse the spouse, is it not?" Santo's Uncle Renaldo put it triumphantly. Renaldo, who was very religious, scoured Scripture to absolve Santo. "The Bible clearly says that Eve was made out of Adam's rib. How can you abuse your own rib? The idea is ridiculous." Still, people talked, and the business had been affected.

Juan brusquely ordered big Santo to bring out six good roasts, if he had such a thing, and to line them up on the counter. Santo silently did this, hoping that Maera would not notice the one Choice among the Prime. But Juan fell on it like an eagle with fish under claw.

"How do you stay in business selling this ratbait?" he asked as he shoved it aside.

Santo said nothing, although he changed color and his gorilla-broad chest began to heave deeply. Juan examined the remaining roasts with the care a surgeon might give to checking a heart for transplant. He eyeballed them, prodded them intimately, and finally, smelled them searchingly. He abruptly pushed a second to the side, with an expression of steely contempt, after his thumb discovered a faint blue imprint.

"This is supposed to be prime beef, not prime tumor," he said.

Santo stood with his arms folded, thinking how much he hated Juan Maera. In fact, he had always hated him, going all the way back to St. Rita's Parochial School, when he used to beat Juan up. It was partly because of his appalling family and his great grades, but the true red flag had been Maera's mind. Twenty years before, Santo would come home from school complaining to his Uncle Renaldo about him: "Whenever I speak in class, Juan Maera looks as though he thinks I'm stupid." Or, "Today I told the class that I have a special devotion to the Virgin. And I told about how I saw Our Lady's face in a yam fritter at the market, and Juan Maera laughed."

"Break his nose," advised Uncle Renaldo. And Santo had. But now they were adults, and it had come to this: Juan Maera had the do-re-mi, and others had to dance to his tune.

With agonizing slowness, Juan also selected two filets of sole, standing over Santo while he trimmed them. Finally, after long hesitation, and with a look of black suspicion, he bought a pork loin. "Might as well die of trichinosis as anything else," he said as he threw bills down on the counter.

When Juan stood on the sidewalk, he realized that he'd left a bag of grapes on the counter. He re-entered the shop. Evidently, Santo was in the meat-cutting room. As Juan picked up his bag, he heard Renaldo:

"That trashy gypsy, he must always flash his money and insult the meat. You would think he would be content with ruining your marriage."

"Maybe I shouldn't have hit Linda," Santo said heavily. "It made her really mad."

"Hit?" Renaldo sounded doubtful. "It was only once, a nudge, a loving correction. You were just schooling her a little, as a good husband must do."

Santo was silent. It was true he'd hit Linda just once, but she'd shattered the aquarium when she slammed into it. He missed her and the children terribly.

Renaldo continued, speaking his hashed and rehashed thoughts in a dogged undertone. "It's as though Maera can't believe the pork is fresh unless he sees me cutting the hog's throat before his eyes. And I feel sick when he puts his hands on my meat. God knows where they've been. People say he has a woman hidden away somewhere. I say a pretty boy is more like it. No wonder his poor old mother died of grief in the asylum. You saw the way he was working his hips when he left the shop. I wish he *would* die from the meat. I would dance and sing, even if it ruined us. It would be worth it."

Juan laughed. The voice abruptly stopped. Juan saw a half dollar in the dark shadows under the counter. He palmed it triumphantly and left the shop.

After a minute, Santo slowly emerged from the meat-cutting room, and walked to the front door. His bull shoulders filled it completely. He looked down the street. During the twenty minutes in which no customers entered the shop, he watched. And he remembered. Lately there had been a serious push among merchants to gentrify the neighborhood. A few weeks back, after considerable discussion with his uncle and serious thought, Santo had bought two hanging basket and arranged them outside. But this did not help. Nothing did. His shop looked like what it was a very short step from the abattoir.

"Interesting," Juan had said when he first saw the baskets. "Sort of like weaving a daisy chain around the horns of a dead bull as it's dragged from the arena."

Now, Renaldo came to stand behind Santo in the doorway. Expressionlessly he watched as Maera stopped at the expensive little specialty shops, buying, always buying.

"You know," he said casually, "I heard that Maera has been advising Linda about good divorce lawyers." Santo was silent, but Renaldo saw his neck redden and swell. Renaldo took out the knife he always carried in his hip pocket, switched it open, and began cleaning meat tissue from under his fingernails.

"A man who acts like that," he said softly, his eyes on the blade, "an atheist who invades the home, he needs to be taught better. It could not be a sin to point out his error. A man, a husband, might even find it necessary to cut him a little, just for his own good, to let out the bad blood."

Juan Maera headed toward the parking lot. Santo stood motionless. "You know," Renaldo said in a quiet voice, "it's the duty of a husband and father to keep his family out of the devil's fist."

After a long moment, Santo said, "I have an appointment I forgot about. I'll be gone all afternoon. Close the store at eight."

He threw some items in a backpack. He hesitated, then tidily rolled up his butcher's apron and also put it in the pack. He left the shop and walked down the street to his old car.

〉〉〉〉

"How is she?" Juan asked. He was standing in the cool hall of an exquisite little stone house. The air was sweetly scented with peach potpourri. The house was only a fifteen-minute drive from his own neighborhood, and he was still fascinated by the magical completeness with which nothing here could be known there.

Mrs. Gonzalez shook her head. "Mr. Maera," she said softly, "your mother is happy, but even less clear in her mind. Of course, she has never been the same since your papa—" and she fell tactfully silent.

On an Ash Wednesday twenty years before, Alma Maera returned early from the market because she'd forgotten certain Lenten preparations for her household. She found a masked intruder slowly cutting her husband's throat. Evidently, Pepe had surprised him in a burglary attempt.

When Juan was located at the library, shepherding his younger brothers and sisters, a look of pure astonishment crossed his face. "Somebody was trying to rob *us*?" he said.

It was well known that Pepe Maera had been a thriftless drunk who savagely beat his wife and children. Everyone thought his death was a good riddance. Any reasonable woman would have thanked God for it on her knees, fasting. However, Pepe had been the first and only man in Alma Maera's life. The marriage may have been an evil enchantment, but she lost her reason incurably mourning it.

Juan had always had an excellent relationship with reality, but to this day, there were certain scenes from his childhood which, for the sake of his sanity, he did not allow himself to recall. Sometimes they flashed on him unaware. For example, he still avoided his reflection in shop windows because then he would see the limp, which, he thought, always made people look at him curiously, trying to figure out exactly what was wrong; what had gone wrong. He hated to recall, now, the years he had spent trying to walk away from that limp.

After Pepe was murdered, a social worker made the Maera children undergo the grief counseling which was just becoming fashionable. As part of a psychological test, fourteen-year-old Juan was asked what word he would use to describe his life with Pepe. "Airborne," he said.

First, Juan put the meat and fruit in the refrigerator. Next, he went to the upstairs hall. Outside his mother's room was a small table on which stood a heavy, magnificent cut-glass bowl, the one relic of her happy childhood home. Not even Pepe had dared to pawn or smash it. Juan opened one of the bags he'd brought, and filled the bowl to overflowing with candy bars. They were mostly Mounds bars, because his mother loved them. However, she could not quite enjoy them with a clear conscience. She thought that coconut and dark chocolate were a luxurious indulgence so pleasurable that they must cross the border into carnal sin.

The first day of Lent, Mrs. Maera ceremoniously put the cut-glass bowl with its candy into a cupboard. Then she wrapped purple gauze scarves around the face of Jesus on the household crucifixes. She had always done this. She explained to Juan that because candy was delicious, and the face of Jesus was lovely to look upon, one must deny oneself during Lent. "I only forgot to do it once," she told him. "And look what happened!"

Juan thought vaguely to himself that Lent was due one of these days. He would have to check the date and stop buying candy bars, or they'd be sitting in the bowl for forty days.

Next, Juan examined some landscaping work he'd had done in the yard, and the little stone-flagged patio leading off the living room. Lush new plantings turned the area into the small Eden he'd envisioned. Above the patio, his mother's balcony had been transformed into a sweet baroque effusion with curly new ironwork. Sometimes she liked to sit out there at night.

Juan minutely examined every plant, every blade of ornamental grass, pebble, and stone he'd paid for. As he did this, he frowned at the harsh growl of an old unmuffled car passing the house. He had paid with big chunks of his life, only he knew how much, to bring his mother to a place where engines purred along as sweetly as a run of good luck.

In the main, he was pleased with the landscaping, but he scowled at a huge rock which was situated under his mother's balcony. The rock was in exactly the wrong spot. Five years before, Alma Maera had had a heart attack. What if this happened on the balcony? He had a horrifying mental image of her falling over the railing, dashing her brains out on the rock below.

He found a steel rod in the garage and was grimly attempting to lever the rock elsewhere, straining and cursing, when Mrs.
Gonzalez stuck her head out the patio door. "Mr. Maera," she
said gently, "your mother is asking for you."

Juan looked unhappily at the rock, but after a minute dropped
the steel rod and re-entered the house. As he closed the door, he
again heard the harsh vibration of the old car, re-passing the
house. Well, that was just fucking great. Undoubtedly it was
some murderous thug planning to rob them blind, carve them
into human gumbo, and leave their carcasses to be discovered
during the first hot spell in June.

Juan walked into the bathroom and made certain adjust-
ments to his appearance, as he always did. He rinsed his face
with cool water, combed his hair sleekly back, and put on a
checked sports jacket. He looked in the mirror for a long minute, his face hard.

His mother was sitting by the fireplace in the living room,
wearing a lilac brocade dress, serenely holding a tomcat wrapped
in a baby blanket. On especially confused days, she thought the
cat was her baby. She would cradle it with the exquisite care of
a Madonna. The tomcat was old, and took this philosophically.
Still, Juan had had it declawed as a precaution.

Beside her on a small table was a picture of a bridal
couple, dressed in the style of forty years back. The dark,
smoothly handsome man—some would have said, a beautiful
man—bent in a romantic and protective posture over his bride.
Her little face, grave and glowing at the same time, looked
directly into the camera. Their two hands were raised, joined,
and bound about with a crystal rosary. The picture was framed
in curly rococo silver. She asked for so few things, but she
had asked for that. Juan seldom looked at this picture. He had
never been able to resign himself that he looked so much like
his father.

The cat yowled. Juan thought that the sight of the dark-eyed
old lady gently jogging her prick-eared hairy bundle, in the time-

less maternal gesture, was lovely, if you could just get over your idea of what a human being should act like. However, he quietly removed the cat and gave it to Mrs. Gonzalez to take away.

Mrs. Gonzalez had restrained Alma's exuberantly curly white hair into a high-dressed corona of braids. Left to herself, she wore it in the fat lovelocks of her youth.

"You look like Queen Isabella," he said. She smiled, and shyly extended her foot a few inches beyond the hem of her skirt, so he could see the lilac pump which matched her dress. She waited a few beats, then with a little ripple of pleasure on her face, anticipating his surprise, she opened a drawer and produced a lilac brocade clutch purse. As he held it and admired it, he noticed that it was empty, and made a mental note to give Mrs. Gonzalez money to buy a gold compact, lipstick, and lace handkerchief for the purse.

He put the velvet box containing the diamond in her hand. "What are you thinking of?" she said, trying to sound severe. "You spend far too much money."

He opened the box and took the jewel from its silk nest. With his other hand, he opened her palm. Slowly, with concentration, he drew the cool stone the length of her lifeline, then up and down its fine tributaries. "There's good fortune for you," he said, "a long life, riches, and I even see a dark, fascinating man."

She laughed. "You know that is all nonsense," she said, with shining eyes.

"Not at all," he said seriously. "I am your good fortune."

She chose to prepare the fish for dinner. Alma Maera had always been a good cook, but her mental illness had turned her into a magnificently adventurous one. Juan had no idea if the perfect sole fillets he'd carved out of Santo's hide would appear classically grilled with almonds, poached with apricot preserves and pistachios, or drenched in salsa with a side of garlicky mashed potatoes.

"They say fish is brain food," she told him earnestly, as she did about once a week, "and lately there have been one or two little lapses . . ."

After dinner, they sat in the living room and watched a DVD. Juan had selected hundreds of films, some of them foreign classics he would dearly have liked to see again. He scrupulously described the choices likely to interest her. She considered this one and that one, compared their merits, and ended by saying thoughtfully, "I really think that we should watch an American movie, to improve my English. I like that one with the friends living together in the old house, they dance and sing all the time, and that black-haired *borracho* reminds me so much of my Uncle Ernesto—"

For the fortieth time that year, Juan put Animal House on the DVD player, and settled back to watch the demented frat men delight his mother. John Belushi did look exactly like Uncle Ernesto, and acted like him, too. Juan did not regret his mother's choice too much. Besides, every once in a while she would ask for a Rita Hayworth movie. Long ago, she'd learned that Hayworth's real name was Margarita Cansino.

As always, Mrs. Maera watched the toga party segment in Animal House with wistful fascination. "Anglos have so much fun," she said, sighing. Mrs. Gonzalez, who was sewing, noted an intent expression on Juan's face after Alma said this. Apparently he was trying to think of some way he could give his mother a toga party. After a minute, the look went away, and she knew he had concluded he could not.

Finally the movie was over, and it was Alma Maera's bedtime. Juan read in the living room as Mrs. Gonzalez brushed his mother's hair and helped her into her convent-made nightdress. After a few minutes, Juan suddenly heard an uproar coming from her room, shrieks, furniture pushed about, a crash and a struggle. His first horrified thought was that an intruder had somehow gotten in through her balcony. As he started to run up the stairs, his bad leg gave way, and he wildly dragged himself upward by the railing, trying to think of something he could use as a weapon. Suddenly his mother appeared in the hallway. Her unbraided white curls bolted exuberantly from her head, and she had thrown a sheet dashingly over her old-fashioned gown. "To-ga!" she said hopefully. "Toga!"

Mrs. Gonzalez came out of the bedroom, slightly disheveled, a determinedly patient look on her face. "Now, Mrs. Maera," she said, and gently led her away.

After a few minutes, Juan went into his mother's room to say good-night. "She insists on sleeping with the toga," Mrs. Gonzalez whispered, "I can't get it away from her."

"Let her be," Juan said.

She was quietly tucked into bed, her hands clasped on the white lace coverlet. My sixty-five-year-old child, Juan thought to himself. He made the sign of the cross on her forehead, as she had always done when he was a boy, kissed her cheek, and was about to leave when she seized his hand.

"Pepe," she said, "have I ever told you how much I admire the way you changed your life? I always knew you were a fine person underneath, but now everyone knows it."

After a minute Juan said, "Thank you, Alma." Then he left the room.

〉〉〉〉

Juan had a date that evening. And he thought, he hoped, from many signs, that tonight might be the night. But he had looked forward to this event for so long, and with such intensity, that he was afraid.

He called and told the person, yawning, that he'd become interested in an article he was reading, and would be an hour late.

There was a silence. Then Siobhan Reilly said, "That's fine, because I needed more time to work on your lesson. Tonight we will study Transubstantiation. We will use certain classic texts—Cardinal Newman, Father Hopkins—I really think," and she could not quite conceal the vibrant hopefulness in her voice, "these brilliant minds will lift you past the doubts you still feel—"

Juan, who had decided by the age of eight that a God who did not help was a God of no use, listened to her ravings with deep affection. He had loved Siobhan Reilly since they were teenagers, although he guarded this secret with the same stubborn care with which he covered his crippled leg. For years he'd tried everything he knew to make her like him too. He even played the clown in her store, just to exist before her eyes. Finally, a few months back, out of absolute desperation, he told her he felt certain tinglings in his long-dead limbs of faith. He begged her to teach him her religion. It had worked. His soul drove her wild. Siobhan saw it as a glorious, elusive fish long submerged in darkest sea-bottom. How passionately she worked to heave it to clear, sparkling water! But, so far, she'd drawn the line at being seen in public with Juan Maera the atheist. They studied late, in a room at the church.

Now Juan drew a deep breath. He thought, This is it. He said casually, "By the way, I'm starving, I haven't eaten all day. Let's meet at a restaurant—Pedro's, say. It's quiet, and we can read while I eat—it won't really be a date, we'll be studying—" He stammered a little, and was furious with himself.

The silence that followed was long indeed. Suddenly he felt them as intolerable, all the years of waiting. And she did not even want to be seen eating a bowl of soup with him. He said roughly, "Oh, let's forget it, I'm too tired anyway—" His disappointment hardened his voice.

"No!" she cried out involuntarily, as she saw the blazing gold soul-fish flash away. Another silence followed. Juan put his cheek to the receiver, begged to it, prayed to it. Come on, my sweet darling, he thought. You can do it.

"Yes," Siobhan said at last, warmly, sounding a little surprised at herself. "We will meet at Pedro's. I will read Cardinal Newman to you as you eat."

Juan spiked his clenched fist into the air, eyes shining.

He showered. Slowly, he opened packages of new clothes and shoes he'd bought, held them up, and examined them minutely. Fumbling a little, he put on khakis as pale and fresh as new wheat, a pinstripe oxford shirt of pristine blue, and a tie. The boat shoes gleamed like buckeyes. He'd also bought a cologne called Eau Sauvage at what he considered terrible expense. He smelled the cap doubtfully. He feared it was so brutally musky she would think he planned to leap on her like a raging beast.

Regretfully, he put the bottle away.

He still had a half hour to wait. "I will relax," he said aloud, in the tone of a man willing to try anything once. Slowly he poured a glass of brandy, and adjusted the lamp. He sat on the big, taupe suede sofa and tried to find the most comfortable spot.

Outside, shadows deepened from rose to purple to black.

For some reason, he could not settle. He felt the way he always felt, that there was something of burning urgency he needed to attend to. He went carefully over the long list of jobs for the day. They had all been accomplished. Still he was uneasy. House sounds seemed heightened or peculiar, and birds in the paradisal little copses in the darkening yard called with almost hysterical insistence.

Juan laughed dryly at himself. The truth, he decided, was that he stank at relaxation. He did not know how to do it. He had to work like a dog at idling. When he tried to smell the roses, he strained every nerve until it cracked.

Also, he thought, looking around, there was definitely something the matter with the placement of the new sofa. It was too far away from the little chandelier. He couldn't believe he had agreed to a location so execrable. He might as well fix it now.

With relief he put the brandy down. He walked around the sofa, planning the best point of attack, then slammed his shoulder into its slab side, and, almost on his knees, pushed until his gut ached. His bad leg buckled. What had possessed him, he wondered, to buy such a fucking big bison of a sofa? It was a monster, a Brahma bull. He braced his leg and tried again. Sweating, cursing, heels dug in, fingers clamped in a deathgrip in the upholstery, he passionately heaved forward. The sofa began to move, inch by inch.

Far back in the dense shadows of the yard, Santo watched with interest. He had to suppress an impulse to offer help.

He'd spent several hours drinking in a bar. Then he'd come back to the Maeras' neighborhood, after dark. He had simply staggered over the low stone wall bordering their property, slashed open one of the artful new arrangements of giant shrubs and vines, forced his way in, and hauled the still green carcass of the copse shut behind him. The great bulk of his shoulders was cloaked in torn wisteria vines, sliced giant lilies, and moonflowers as beautiful as a dream.

He knew he was very drunk, but not too drunk to get the job done. A knife was as natural to his hand as its fingers. Alcohol washed through him, a languorous burn. He felt that his lobes and arteries shone scarlet through black clothes, black mask. Behind it, his eyes tracked Juan's movements as a gorilla might idly follow the comings and goings of a busy little rodent who is absorbed in successfully arranging his world. The rodent goes here and there, pleased with his tidy accomplishments. He thinks that he holds his little life in his hands. But actually it is the gorilla, with his sardonic deadpan, who knows the rodent's true destiny very well.

Santo remembered what his uncle had said. He prayed briefly to the Virgin, asking her to protect him as he defended his home. Then he put on his bloodstained apron with economical,

workmanlike movements. The handle of his favorite knife sat
sweetly in his hand.

Alma Maera woke bolt upright. Her temples drummed with
warnings, the sable night air swarmed with angel alarms.

Oh, people did not understand angels. Angels were not soft
and sweet, rage blazed in their flight. They forgave nothing, not
the smallest lapse. They jammed coals of warning in your ears,
dragged you by the hair of your head up and down the gran-
ite steps of the house of truth. Now they were screaming that
she had once again forgotten a task of desperate importance, an
omission so deadly that it opened the palms, feet, and side of her
family to the cruelest thrusts. Now what—

Alma dropped her head in her hands. Desperately, she cast
for a date, a day. Nobody knew how she could do this, there
wasn't a calendar in the house because she became so upset as
Lent approached. But four seasons wheeled on green streams of
leaves through her head, glimmered in angles of the moon, she
counted on her fingers, prayed numbers, calculated which fruit
blossoms she was smelling, the texture of the silky night air—

She caught the day and sprang from her bed crying out. The
clock said 11:58 p.m.

She thought wildly, *I have no time.* She ran to her bureau and
pawed through the lowest drawer, pulling out the shimmering
emblems she needed.

The iron angel voices spoke again. They said sternly, *Do not
tarry. Go to the balcony and save your best beloved.*

Juan had the sofa where he wanted it. Now he would have his
brandy. He walked to the alcove where the drinks table was located, his back to the patio.

Santo walked out of the copse, not bothering to conceal himself, destroyed vines and flowers clinging to his legs and shoulders. He walked directly to the patio door, his eyes on Juan's back,
when a sound above made him look up.

A little figure robed in white stood on the balcony. Racing stars seemed to fly in the wind with the purple scarves whipping banner-like from her shoulders. In her arms, she cradled a rounded object. From head to lace hem she shimmered softly in the moonlight, and moonlight turned the coronet of her hair to a halo. She seemed to have no feet.

Santo stood still, poleaxed. Then, with a great effort, his stunned limbs moved. He approached her slowly, his fascinated eyes never leaving her. *It is She,* he thought. *Just like the picture in   the church!* A great sob of wonder and adoration lodged like a fist in his throat. He forgot about his mask, the knife in his hand. He put one boot on the rock beneath the balcony, wrapped his free hand in its grill work, and began to pull himself up. He wanted to kiss her hem.

She looked at the man clad in garments of blood, at his black-masked face and raised knife. In his whole giant figure, the only living tissue which showed was the red-shot whites of his eyes. "Why, Santo Rivera!" she said, in surprise.

Santo almost fell off the rock. *The Mother of God knows me,* he thought in stupefaction.

Now she was looking so pointedly at the knife in his hand that he looked at it too, as if wondering how it got there. "Santo," she said, with a note of steel in her voice, "what have you come to do to these poor Maeras?"

Santo hung his huge shaggy head and blushed painfully behind his mask. "I was only going to stick him a little," he mumbled, then was horrified to realize he had just lied to the Virgin. She, who knew everything, would know very well that he'd planned to cut Juan Maera's head clean off.

"Shame on you, Santo!" she said fiercely. "For shame!"

Our Lady is mad at me, he thought in terror. He looked covertly at the ten-inch blade in his hand, trying to think of some way to make it disappear. On a desperate inspiration, he modestly hiked up his pant leg a few inches, inserted the knife in his boot, neatly patted the pants cuff down smooth and looked up, trembling, for approval.

"That's much better, Santo," she said warmly. "You must never harm a hair of his head. Now go home."

Weeping, swaying, Santo reached upward. He was determined to kiss her hem, no matter what. He thought, *I will never get another chance.* As he moved, the great gong of whiskey in his head slammed back and forth and he began to fall. He desperately grabbed for a holdfast, his fingers closed on the glittering glass bowl in her arms, and he pulled it and a blizzard of candy bars down crashing with him to the stone flags.

It was too much. Santo screamed, thrashed in his own blood in a frenzy, then fought upright and bolted away, half dead with shock. Two mighty bounds and he hit the sidewalk, running so hard he was afraid his guts would pop out of his mouth. The Virgin had told him to go home, and he was going home. But even then, some part of his mind wondered what the sticky little objects were that clung to his knees along with shards of glass.

Juan turned when he heard the screams, but could see nothing in the dark yard except a rush of movement, as of a giant dog, clearing the low stone wall. In the next instant he heard the balcony door slam upstairs, then his mother came running out of her room and down the stairs, dexterously unwinding purple scarves as she came. "A mad beast," she gasped out as she flashed past, "nothing important, no time to talk."

Zigzagging through the rooms, her white nightdress a wildly billowing comet's tail as she ran, she cast a skein of shimmering gauze over each of the seven crucifixes in the living room, dining room, and kitchen, remembered a new one she'd forgotten on the landing, bolted frantically back upstairs, ensnared it in a web of purple, and then suddenly was done.

As she stood motionless, panting, her hands flung wide like a bulldogger who has successfully tied his steer, the clock struck midnight.

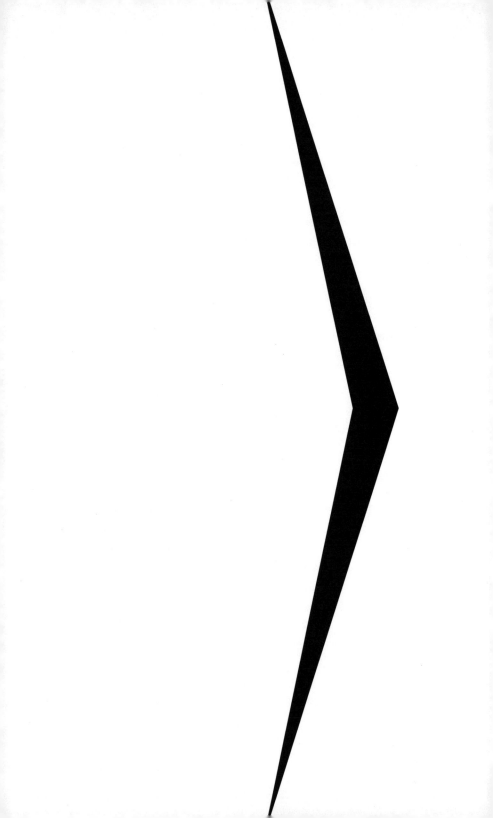

SIMEON PROPHET AND JOHANNA

The painting was no good, and Simeon didn't know why. It had the best of all subjects, his wife Georgie. It had a fine title: *Unique Is My Dove*. He'd worked hard, straight through three days and three nights. By the end of the third night, he could barely see. On the back of the canvas he wrote in clumsy letters, *All my being is aglow, waiting for one who does not come*. Georgie had been dead and buried for four months.

It made sense to him that night to slash his left palm and write these words in his blood. Then he fell asleep as though he'd been hit on the back of the head with a shovel.

When he finally woke up, late in the afternoon of the next day, he was frightened to see what he'd done. He knew his mind didn't always work quite right since Georgie died, but never before had he written in blood. *Save me, Jesus.* He promised himself he wouldn't do it again, no matter what.

He made strong coffee, then sat down and looked at the painting. He decided that the problem was an emptiness, right by the ankle-straps of Georgie's favorite shoes, where her cat Roy belonged. Since the cat was diabetic and weighed at least thirty pounds, and had red-gold fur that stood up all over, his absence was considerable. It was as though the fat dwarf was missing in one of those ancient paintings of Spanish royal families that Simeon admired. Roy wasn't where he should be. After Georgie died, the animal had taken to disappearing, skidding out the door like grease through a goose. He liked to escape to the park, torment and eat up any wildlife that couldn't fight him off.

Sighing, Simeon put his jacket on and headed toward the park.

〉〉〉〉

Both men and boys belonged to the Satan's Lords. Today, several of them were by the fountain, playing their death-zombie music. Jason Koben was with them, had been for two years now, ever since his mother died. Simeon walked in the other direction. He kept his head turned away. They watched him.

He searched among the pines where he'd found Roy before. Suddenly he spotted a big heaving glare of color, a human effigy-mound which he knew all too well, under a distant oak. Simeon swore to himself. Yes, there was the woman-mountain Johanna, wrapped in a red cloak. Her dense black curls sprang up and out, forming a noble orb. She sat bolt upright in her scarlet cloak on her sunflower comforter with the authority of a czarina. There was the baseball bat, handy to her fist, with which she defended her space and her safety. And there was Roy, enthroned upon her mighty knees.

Johanna gestured to Simeon imperiously. He felt the first flashing prongs of a headache coming at him. He tried to meet it with steel. He told himself he would control his temper no matter what Johanna said or did. Sometimes she became belligerent and used language that would knock a buzzard off a shithouse. More important, she had once destroyed the best picture he ever painted, in a drunken rage. He hadn't forgotten it, and he never would. But today he would give it no mind. He remembered what Father Karl had said in church the Sunday before: "Cast out your demons and go about your business with a glowing face, as though they weren't even a bump in your road."

Simeon walked slowly up to Johanna. Now that he was closer, he could see that around her neck she wore an enormous cross, braided from red, yellow, and blue yarn. *Trust her to supersize it*, he thought. There were a few crackling wrappers of candy bars and Frito Scoopers on the comforter, but he noticed with surprise that the usual mounds of brandy bottles and trash were gone.

Roy was sprawled out, his furry red belly upward, on the gypsy-red folds of her skirt. Simeon looked greedily at him. The cat glittered like a powerful holy image cast in bronze. He was gently mumbling some object in his mouth. Simeon came closer, and could see that it was the head of a baby rabbit. *Oh my sweet Jesus God*, the man thought. He took a deep breath, trying to get his gorge back where it belonged.

"I'm real glad you found my cat," Simeon said, choosing his words carefully. "I'll just take him off your hands now."

"You mean this cat here?" Johanna said. She stared at the thirty-pound tom lounging on her knees, slobbering rodent blood and tissue, as though noticing him for the first time.

"Yes, my Roy. You've been real kind, but I need him for a picture and I'll take him home now."

"Well," she said, "he's not your cat. He's mine. Georgie gave him to me on her deathbed."

At this outrageous lie, Simeon snapped. "She did not!"

"She did. You weren't around that afternoon, so you didn't hear her. She was just talkin' into my private ear." Johanna spoke very slowly and clearly, as though to an idiot.

"Everybody on our street knows that's my cat!"

"Well, they'd better not say so," Johanna scowled. Simeon had an apocalyptic vision of their poor but quiet block littered with slashed tires, the diamond shards of shattered windows, and an almighty stink of roofs crowned with cat feces. Johanna the destroyer would be striding triumphantly away with her red cloak flapping and the monstrous red cat clawed tight to her mane.

Simeon had a sudden, powerful impulse to pick up a rock and bash Johanna over the head with it. Immediately he was horrified at himself. They'd only been talking for forty seconds. *Forgive me, Jesus.*

"Simeon, you'd better sit down, you look real poorly," Johanna said with concern. She moved the Moon Pie wrappers aside and patted the comforter. Roy yowled and resettled himself in her lap, lazily lipping the bunny head. "I promised Georgie I'd look after you, but I've just been so busy…I'd planned to come by again and cut you up more wood, because your woodpile is so low. If you're going to be so backward as to use that awful old wood stove, at least you ought to keep it up. And have you been eating right?"

Uneasily, Simeon remembered the week before, when he'd caught Johanna in his back yard, cutting wood for him by moonlight. It had been a sight to behold. She went after that wood like there was no tomorrow. The black shock waves of her hair whipped back and forth. Around her swooping bulges she'd pinned a length of purple brocade like a toga. That woman's curves were ungodly. In her purple she looked like his Bible picture of Queen Jezebel chasing hellbent after the holy prophets. Standing in the yard, Simeon thought: *Jezebel cracked the pussy whip over those prophets until they barked like dogs.* Then he was so shocked at this lewd thought that he threw Johanna off his property immediately. She'd looked set to chop wood all night, too.

Now Simeon wondered with piercing grievance why it was that Georgie, who loved beauty, had been compelled to befriend this maddening hag. Although, to be fair, Johanna looked better than she used to. In the past, she'd needed a damned good scrubbing all over, and she seemed to have gotten it. She smelled better, he decided, breathing in cautiously. She smelled like soap and strong flowers.

"I'll pay for his board," Simeon said, reaching for his wallet. "I'll—I'll—"

"It's not about the money," Johanna said, "it's whether you're in shape to take good care of him. He's used to the best. I've given him Chicken of the Sea tuna." She pointed to cans in a nearby bush. "I don't know what kind of junk you been feeding him, but his diabetes was off the charts when I got him. Now he's better. And I've carried him around like my baby boy." She rifled through a neatly stacked pile of goods and held up an infant sling, only a little battered, made out of exotic oriental fabric. "I've given him the run of my home—"

Simeon snapped again. "You don't have a home!" he shouted. "You're homeless!"

"I do so," she said proudly. "I had Lloyd arrested for abusing me and got him kicked out and took over his place. I just come here for the fresh air."

Simeon gaped. Johanna's husband Lloyd was no more than half her size. She'd once overturned a refrigerator on him. If he'd hit her, it must have been when she had her boot on his neck and he was flailing in terror. Simeon gave it up.

"I need Roy to be in a picture of Georgie," he said flatly.

Johanna's gaze shot up into the sky and searched it. Her hand gripped the cross at her neck. After a minute she said quietly, "Maybe it's a sign. I've been praying to Georgie to help me do better."

Simeon was dead sure it was sacriligeous to pray to a human. Father Karl would be furious. But he could feel the cat within his grasp, so he didn't tell her so. Instead, he said, "That's—that's good. So you'll bring Roy over tonight?"

She promised, and Simeon turned to leave. Out of the corner of his eye he could see that the Satan's Lords were now closer, by the benches no more than fifty yards distant. One of them was walking away, leaving the park. Although Simeon saw him only from the back, once again he recognized Jason Koben. Nobody else had the word MAMA cut into his head.

Everything in that family had gone to hell when the mother died. He'd sent the children a memorial portrait of her, because Sarah Koben had been his friend. She'd been one of the students in his art class at the community center. But now Sarah was dead, and her oldest boy, Jason, the one who'd been so bright and promising, was a Satan's Lord—a high-up one, judging by the way the others deferred to him. Simeon shivered. How could it be so? Only a few years back, that kid had been singing in the gospel choir in a shirt so white it hurt your eyes.

I didn't used to be afraid, Simeon thought. But now he was getting older, and he'd heard that the Satan's Lords were the worst yet. They beat old people half to death and tortured bums and had lit up a cat. It seemed they didn't have any mercy. They'd hit a woman as if she were a man.

"Johanna, you best be careful of those Satan's Lords," he said, turning back. "They're real hateful. And I heard they—they treat ladies like they ought not to do."

"I know," she said. She looked at the men. She pointed to the biggest. "That's Gulden, he's the worst. He hurt Marsha. He hurt her bad." Marsha was Johanna's friend, a schizophrenic woman who used to sleep in the park. Johanna looked steadily at Gulden. She said, "Somebody needs to slow him down real good."

"You best take Roy and go home right now. They could hurt you too, Johanna."

"Who, *them?*" she said contemptuously. "It's not true for my life. I'm under holy protection. It ain't gonna happen." She lifted Roy and gently set him on a nest of baby blankets. She found an empty brandy bottle in a nearby bush. She seized it by the neck, raised her great brawny arm, and smashed the bottle down on a rock. Then she gripped her baseball bat in one hand and held the jagged bottle aloft in the other, scowling toward the men. They looked at her.

"I got it well in hand," she said.

Simeon nodded and walked away, trying not to hurry. He was trembling, and hoped Johanna didn't notice. When he'd walked around the row of pines and out of her eyesight, he stepped out for home through the park as fast as he could. Still, he saw that two of the boys had detached from the others and were drifting toward him. One of them was Gulden. Then Simeon knew that no matter how fast he tried to move, it would not be fast enough.

They could take what was his and strike him down on a whim. They would steal his money for sure. They might gouge his eyes and cripple the hands that he painted with. It was in their power. All he could hope was that they were too tired or drunk or strung out to hurt him badly. He could not stop them by any manner of means, and so he had to endure it.

When Simeon finally reached his home, he had to steady his right hand with his left to put the key in the door. Inside, he stood in the middle of the studio, shaking. He walked over to the little mirror above the bookcase and looked at his face. He couldn't see any bruises, but then, he could hardly see at all in the dark. After a minute, he walked away from the mirror.

He thought briefly of calling the police, but those boys had said, *We know where you live*, and they did. He'd better quit while he still had his eyes and his hands.

What he wanted to do was turn the lights on, make strong coffee, then take his charcoal and pencils and draw the Satan's Lords. He'd gotten through what happened by concentrating on the details of their eyes and tattoos and clothing. One had a black barbed wire necklace. The other had his own jugular vein outlined up and down with tiny black skulls. Simeon knew that most people would not want to draw those who had robbed and beaten them, but it was all he wanted to do. He couldn't wait to get at it. In particular, he didn't want to forget that grotesque jacket the worst one, Gulden, had been wearing, because it was like nothing he'd ever seen before. But he couldn't make himself turn the light on so that he could see to draw. He was afraid to.

He sat in the dark and thought. *I never used to be a coward.* The studio was icy, but he was even afraid to put a log in the woodstove. *They'll see the glare and come after me.* He couldn't remember when he'd last been so cold. Then he put his mind to it, and he did remember.

Georgie had been buried late on a winter afternoon, dark and snowy, in a country cemetery twenty miles from the city. They had buried her in the hard ground, and because of the way people felt about her, that grave was heaped from head to foot with white flowers. But all he could think of was the six feet of cold dirt underneath, holding her down.

He'd ridden to the service with the undertaker. Afterward, many people had offered him a ride back. Without a tear, harshly, he refused them all. He knew they wondered at his rudeness. He stared them down, fiercely willed them to go. Then he was alone, and somehow he lost the next few hours. When he woke up, he found he'd lain down beside her grave like a dog. He was so cold he thought he was going to die. Slowly, he stood up. It seemed so strange that he could rise and she could not.

He walked all the way home in the frozen dark. He walked past water like a stone. There were some miles where he struck his face and his breast with his fist like a crazy man. Wailing down those cold roads in the dark: it was something he could never forget.

When he'd reached home right before dawn, Johanna was sitting on his doorstep. He knew she'd been there all night. She looked as bad as he felt. She had Georgie's old mohair muffler wrapped around her head, and her woeful face with tears on it peered out, so that somehow that huge woman looked like a hurt little girl. Without a word, he'd walked around her, unlocked the door, went in, and locked it behind him.

The thought of Johanna, and the baseball bat and bottle which were all the protection she had, made him flinch with shame. *A few slaps and they've got me creeping around in the dark, whining and crying like a baby rat eating a red onion.* He stood up and turned the lamps on. *After all, there's not much more they can do to me.* He threw a log into the wood stove. He unlocked the doors, both front and back. *What do you want to take, the little bit of money I've got left? Come and get it. And fuck you.* Then he felt bad, because he'd promised Georgie to always watch his language. But he didn't take it back.

He put the kettle on and made coffee. Then he took his charcoal and pencils and began to draw the Satan's Lords who'd attacked him. His hand almost outran the images in his head. Twenty minutes and there they were in strokes of black and grey, clear as the day the devil formed them. He wondered, in passing, why it was that he could no longer draw Georgie, who was so precious and godly, but these evil ones were alive on his page even to their bone marrow.

He decided to give them red teeth. Let everybody know that they were flesh-eaters. When he couldn't find pencils or paint of the red that he saw in his head, he hesitated only a minute before opening the cut in his left palm and swirling the brush in it. What the hell: at least it would be the right color.

He began to draw their eyes. Most people's eyes were about light, but not these. How could you draw what was not there? He thought, When the eye is bad, the whole body is dark. He crosshatched a blank darkness across their eyeballs.

The picture was turning out so well he was afraid to believe it. Breathlessly, he continued. The big one who'd hit him, the one they called Gulden, had worn a leather jacket so heavy it was like he was carrying around a hunk of animal body instead of the flayed skin. Simeon drew the jacket as a dark wolf corpse draped over Gulden's shoulders and chest, its gaping jaws stretched dead at his neck. But it was Gulden's teeth and jaws, not the wolf's, which he painted red.

And it was with this man and the others that he'd left Johanna in the park. Simeon struggled to ignore this thought, to continue working, but in the end he threw his brush down. *I've got to go help her, and get the shit beat out of me. God damn it to hell.*

He was reaching for his coat, his back to the front door, when he heard someone open it and walk in. Simeon smelled Gulden before he saw him: foul body, musky cologne, and a sharp peppermint reek. When Simeon smelled the angel dust on the man, and saw his eyes, terror forked through him. He thought: *I won't scream, no matter what.* There was no one to help, anyway. He tried feverishly to distract himself, to wrench his mind away from whatever was going to happen to him. He noticed that the big buttons on Gulden's jacket had skull designs he hadn't drawn correctly. He stared at them as the man spoke.

It was something about "everything you have," and a list following. At the same time Simeon was confused by a loud, rhythmic noise outside, sudden battering strikes out back. *More of them coming*, he thought. *Oh Jesus God.* Then: *Just let me live until I can get those buttons right.* He wondered if things would go better or worse for him if Gulden found the drawing. Would he be flattered, think it was like being on television?

"You disrespecting me? You having trouble paying attention?" Gulden drew back his fist, swung it and flattened Simeon's nose. Simeon cried out. He couldn't help it, to his shame. He backed up to the kitchen table.

"You are one sorry-ass coward, you know that? I haven't even done nothing yet." Gulden drew a knife out of his clothes. It was such a casual gesture, as though anywhere he put his hand he could count on a knife sliding into it. He poised the tip of the knife at Simeon's eye. He rested his other hand, which was covered with rings, on the table. "Put your wedding ring—"

But Simeon never knew where Gulden wanted the ring because at that second Johanna bolted into the studio through the back door with red skirts whipping and her brawny arms raised high, an axe clenched in her fists, the enormous red cat screeching after her, and she laid that steel blade down like a judgment across Gulden's fingers. Big flesh chunks popped off. Rings rolled away. Simeon gaped stupidly at the pieces. Roy's fat, solid body, like a red keg with fur, capered happily. He jumped on the table and lapped a little blood.

"You thought he had no friends?" Johanna shouted at Gulden above the sound he was making. "Is that what you thought?"

But loud as they both were, Simeon heard the front door open. He turned and saw Jason Koben walk into the studio. Jason stood still for a minute and took it all in: Johanna and her axe, Gulden's maimed fingers, and Simeon's nose. Simeon was struck by his quietness. He looked as calm as though he'd seen this scene, or one so like it as to make no difference, every day of his life. When he walked forward, Gulden cringed back.

"Gulden, you always were too stupid to live," Jason said. "I told you never to touch him. And stop making that noise." Gulden tried desperately to muffle his moans.

Jason placed a small packet of bills on the table, avoiding the blood puddle. Simeon realized it must be the money that had been stolen from him that afternoon. The boy carefully assessed Simeon's face. He took out his wallet and threw several large bills on top of the packet. "I'm sorry about your nose," he said softly.

"It wasn't your fault."

"But it was my boy that got out of control."

As Jason was settling his debts, Simeon studied him. Unlike the other Satan's Lords, he wore simple black clothes. He had a strong, handsome presence, without swagger. He looked like one of those young princes in ancient portraits, born in plague years and raised in war years: strangers to peace, knowing it and accepting it. Simeon thought that he would have liked to draw him, if it hadn't been such a bad time to bring it up.

Jason put his wallet back in his pocket. He looked around the studio. He said, "I always wondered what it was like in here." As though he were alone, he turned away from them and walked slowly around the room, looking at the pictures. They watched him silently. From this angle Simeon could see the word MAMA cut into his head.

Finally Jason said, "My mom liked being in that art class of yours. She used to say—" he bent closer to a picture, lightly touched the brushwork, "—you must have an angel in your head. And that was a real nice picture you drew of her, when she passed."

He continued his tour. Some pictures he went back to twice. Some he took in his hands so he could study the details. When he reached the sketch of the Satan's Lords, he stared, then laughed. "God, ain't it the truth," he said. He kept looking at it. He pointed to Gulden's teeth and jaws. "Is that real blood?" When Simeon nodded, Jason looked at him a little oddly, but not disrespectfully. He said, "Your picture is like that one." He pointed to a Goya print on the wall. It was a charcoal drawing from the series called *Disasters of War*, and showed soldiers grinning as one of them tortured a peasant.

"Can I have it?" Jason said. He pointed to the picture of the Satan's Lords. When Simeon said nothing, Jason turned around and looked at him. It was only a look, but for the first time Simeon thought, *He's one of them. He does what they do. And I'm damn lucky his ma was my friend.*

"Yes," Simeon said. He watched sorrowfully as Jason rolled up the second best picture he'd ever drawn. Johanna had destroyed the best months before.

Jason stood with the drawing in his hand and looked back at the other pictures, one by one. He said to Simeon, "You are damn fucking good." He spoke with a grim, almost cold admiration. Simeon thought how strange it was that in all his years of work, the compliment that meant the most to him came from a gangbanger.

"Gulden, we got to go to the Emergency. Stop whining and collect your goddamn finger stumps and let's get out of here. Mr. Prophet, do you have an old Baggie somewhere and a little ice?"

Johanna located a Baggie, but the finger pieces themselves were hard to find. Eventually two turned up in the dust under the kitchen table. Roy was sitting on top of the refrigerator mumbling the third in his mouth, and they had a hard fight to get it away from him. The fourth they couldn't find at all. Simeon thought that Roy must have already eaten it. Gulden began to lament and curse foully again, until Johanna held the axe to his face. He shut up, clamping his jaws.

Jason said, "She's schooling you like her little dog, Gulden." He looked at Johanna and pointed to the bloody rings on the table . For a moment he had his mother's broad, open smile. "Take your pick," he said. "Thank you for helping Simeon. And I am saying to you that nobody is going to bother you for that."

Johanna scowled fiercely. "I don't need no thanks," she said, "and I don't need no God damned protection." But in the end she selected a carnelian pinky ring and daintily put it on her little finger. Gulden made a muted woeful sound, as loud as he dared.

"Jason," Simeon said, "why don't you get shut of him? Just leave him someplace. Go your way."

"They don't never leave one behind, no matter what," Johanna said to him gently, as though to a child. "You know that."

"You have a lot of life left," Simeon said to Jason.

"I don't," the boy said. Then he and Gulden left, Jason politely catching the screen door so it wouldn't slam behind them.

They were no sooner out the door than Johanna rushed over to lock and bolt it. She burst into a rocketing starburst of tears. She stood tall, swaying violently back and forth like a big red dahlia all of whose petals were shivering, and she cried out with her face and big arms flung upward. "Thank you, thank you Lord Christ, that your sweet Jesus hand took the death shroud from Simeon and let him live!"

His sweet Jesus hand took its damn time, Simeon thought, but aloud he said, "Amen and Amen."

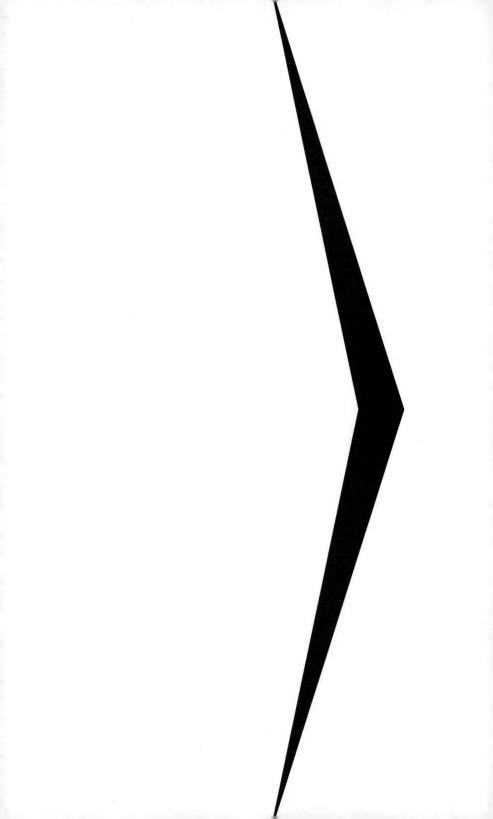

JOE SZABO AND THE GYPSY BRIDE

"Gypsies, Abel," the father said, not bothering to keep his voice down. He glared at them and his fingers worked a Bemberg lining into a coat at the same time.

"How do you know?"

"I know. Look at their hair. Look at their skirts."

Abel looked. He thought their hair and skirts were wonderful. "They sound Irish," he said in a low voice. "And these days you're supposed to call them Travellers."

"I'll call them whatever the hell I want in my own shop. Get them out of here."

The woman and the young girl seemed not to hear him. They quietly talked to each other as they looked about the shop with their long eyes.

Joe Szabo and his son Abel made suits, and had an entirely male clientele. The shelves were filled with bolts of somber tweeds. Joe liked to work with black, navy, banker's grey, and shades of brown. That was it. Once a rich and famous alderman came in cuddling a Pekinese to his cheek. As the alderman gently massaged the tiny dog all over with his forefinger, making it wriggle and sigh, he told Joe that he wanted him to make a tuxedo jacket out of hunting pink, with a matching jacket and bow tie for the little dog.

Joe threw them out of the shop. "Gaybird," he said, under his breath. *Like me, Pop,* Abel thought. *You can't even imagine.* Then Joe stood in the doorway and shouted after them, "You two ought to rent a room!"

Like Aaron and I used to do, Abel thought. *Because if I went to his apartment his other boyfriend might guess about us. And his girlfriend too.* Aloud he said, "I hope you enjoyed that, because it's going to cost us."

"I know," Joe said. "But it was worth it."

Abel said, "I can't believe I dropped out of college to help you." *And I lost Aaron.* "When you put Grandpa in the nursing home, I thought things would go better in the shop. There would no longer be this insane old naked guy wandering into the front room in his truss, terrifying the customers. But I forgot how sometimes you just have to insult people, how you talk to them like a goddamn ape. I forgot how you are, Pop."

"Your mistake," Joe said. "Oh, and I just got another call from the nursing home. Grandpa's in trouble; he tried to jump that nurse again. I told them to get him an uglier nurse." Joe laughed.

"That's not funny. If they kick him out, we're totally screwed."

The older Traveller woman stood arrogantly tall with her hands on her hips, the sides of her fur coat thrown back. Abel could see that her dress of burnt paprika silk was fashioned with tempestuous gores and godets. The young girl wore cerulean blue. The women were a bolt of color against a wall crammed with briary wool in tones of stony fields and winter woods. They both carried rolled-up parcels.

"Talk to them," Joe said. "But don't give them a damned thing."

"They look all right," Abel said. "Do me a favor and don't do your apeshit routine."

"What are you, four years old? They'll rob you if you give them an inch. They'll rob you twice. Get rid of them." Joe turned back to the Bemberg lining, sighing heavily because he'd raised such a fool.

It was the older woman who talked to Abel. She was Irish all right, although her brogue had fine malt whiskey in it rather than the green lilt. She said that her niece Mareid, the girl, was going to get married. They wanted the Szabos to make her wedding dress. They had the yard goods, beautiful fabric, all they needed was the tailors' skill.

Joe shouted rudely from the back of the shop, "We only make men's suits."

The aunt ignored him. She said to Abel, "We will pay you with this." She waited a beat, then smoothly flipped the bundle off her shoulder and unfurled it. Abel saw roses and Arabian ponies and tiny robed people suddenly run over the floor. They were passionately riding, embracing, praying, and fighting. It was all rolled out before him.

"Pop," Abel said.

Joe must have heard something in his voice, because he came right away. The rug was gorgeous, extraordinary. He studied it morosely, and finally found a flaw.

"It's damaged," he said, pointing in triumph to a tiny knick in the border fringe.

Her fine lip curled. "It's a hundred years old," she said. "It's wonderful. Wonderful is better than perfect. Any slave at a machine can give you perfect."

"You think a slave didn't make this rug?" Joe said.

When he said that, she averted her gaze from him as though from a defecating dog. He, however, never took his eyes off her.

As they argued about the rug, Abel looked at the girl. Her hair grew in long, sumptuous black spirals. Aaron's hair grew like that, although his was red. A sunny green fragrance came off her. Abel could understand, sort of, why his Czech grandfather, when he became too senile to care what people thought, used to bite hard on the side of his fist when he saw a beautiful woman.

Finally Joe said, "The rug is not so bad." He sighed morbidly and added, "Maybe you could even mend those mothholes." He pointed to a few specks of dust on a pony's gold mane.

The aunt nodded to the girl. Now it was Mareid's turn to take the bundle off her shoulder and spread it out on the table.

The silk was soft, heavy, and white, with a drape fluid as water, and yet strong, as though it could withstand being wrenched by fists. It had threads of both gold and silver woven into it, a subdued shining. White embroidered garlands swept over the whole piece. Joe couldn't stop himself from touching it.

"Foreign cloth," Joe said. "Probably some Chinese child went blind doing the embroidery. Where's the pattern?"

The aunt rummaged in her bag and brought out a scrap of newspaper, much folded and frayed. It was a publicity photo of Princess Caroline of Monaco at her first wedding. Joe was silent, as though beyond words. Finally he said, "So you're telling me there is no pattern?"

The aunt gave him her contemptuous, damn-your-eyes blue stare. "I thought you were a tailor," she said. "I thought you had skills."

"Pop," Abel said, warning him.

But instead, after a silence, Joe said, "Right." Abel thought, *How did she know she could beat him with a dare?*

"When is the wedding?" Joe said. "I'd like at least two weeks."

"The wedding is tonight," the aunt said indifferently.

"Oh," Joe said, "of course. Naturally." His fist tightened on the fabric. "I need to measure her. Abel, get the tape."

"You can't touch her," the aunt said, staring at his hand as though at a filthy and infected gorilla's paw. "It's not proper. You can measure her by holding the tape a couple inches from her body."

"I would prefer not to make such a fool of myself," Joe said, coldly and evenly. "I can figure out her measurements by looking at her. However, she will have to take off that fur coat."

The aunt looked disgusted, as though he'd made some fantastically gross, inappropriate demand. Abel took over, ushering them with bows and soft words to the fitting room.

When eventually Mareid had taken off her fur coat and even her blue dress, she was still covered, both up and down. She wore a long, loose, sturdy white cotton slip, of the type Abel had always associated with nuns' underwear. She looked like a proud young angel who'd come to light softly for only a minute on those little feet, and would fly off in a heartbeat. Only her bracken-thick mane of black hair looked of the earth.

She was wearing the most beautiful shoes that Abel had ever seen. They were lilac kidskin wedgies with pink silk ribbons that crossed softly over her ankles and up her calves. Abel remembered that Aaron used to laugh at him for liking pink so much. "Such a stereotype. Pink-pank-punk." He was staring at the shoes when he felt his father's eyes on him. Abel raised his gaze and tried to leer at her breasts.

Joe walked around Mareid for no more than fifteen seconds, then without comment wrote down a dozen measurements. "That's it," he said. He nodded curtly to the aunt and left the room. Abel followed him.

When the aunt and girl emerged a few minutes later, the aunt was still frowning. When she spoke, her brogue was more throaty and aggressive than before. "The dress material is as valuable as the rug. I want every scrap back that ye don't use."

"I know you do," Joe said.

"The wedding is at eight," she said. "We will pick the dress up at seven."

Joe walked them to the door. He was already rolling his sleeves up. The aunt said, stating a fact, "It's the big arms like Popeye ye have."

Joe scowled. She put her hand on his bare forearm and looked up at him calmly with her long blue eyes. There was a beauty mole on her neck, swept by black curls. She said, "Sure, there's not a thing the matter with strong Popeye arms."

Then she and Mareid were gone. Like thoroughbreds, they walked down the street on their long legs, climbed into a magnificent white Cadillac, and drove away.

Abel said, "That aunt is not a bad-looking woman."

"Wash her and send her to my tent," Joe mocked. But he still looked shaken.

Abel said, "If you think about it, she's paying us a big compliment by trusting us with this job."

Joe said, "I have thought about it, and she's whipping us like fucking racehorses."

Joe hung up the CLOSED sign. He got on the phone and brusquely cancelled several suit fittings. He was especially rude with the mayor.

"Oh yeah," Abel said, "let's definitely alienate and insult the mayor. What a good idea. Who needs him? Money isn't everything."

Joe said, "The mayor is going to keep coming back because I sew him suits that make his fat ass look like Brad Pitt's."

He looked for a long minute at the photo of Princess Caroline in her dress. He looked at the list of Mareid's measurements, set them aside and spread out the dress material. He eyed it like a burly conquistador gloating over Incan concubines whom he was about to ravish.

"Of course you're going to make a pattern," Abel said.

Joe smoothed the fabric until it was perfectly flat. He grabbed his favorite cutting shears, snapped his neck from side to side as an athlete does to pop the kinks out, and shrugged his big shoulders to loosen them.

"I don't know who you're showing off for," Abel said, "there's only me here. Now make a goddamn pattern for Christ's sake."

"You've seen me cut free-hand before," Joe said. "I see the coat or whatever and I know without thinking what all the pieces should be. I only heard of two others in the world who could do it. Balenciaga, and that English freak who just killed himself, Alexander McQueen. It was just them and me. Pretty rare. Pretty special."

"It's more like being an idiot savant," Abel said. "I wouldn't brag if I were you."

Joe snorted, tightened his grip on the shears, and slashed into the cloth fearlessly. He cut smoothly and rapidly without stopping for five minutes.

Abel said, "I hate when you do that. It's so weird that you can. And you're cutting the pieces too close."

"I'm keeping about a third of the material. For me."

Abel was silent with surprise. His father had always been honest to the point of obsession. He said, "The aunt will know."

"Let her. She thinks I took some? Good luck proving it. What is she going to do, curse me, give me the evil eye?" Joe laughed softly.

"Pop, that's a beautiful rug they're giving us."

"We'll never see that rug again. They'll shove some rolled-up crap into our arms and take off. Those gypsies couldn't stick to a deal if they tried, which they don't. It's not in their blood. Grandpa told me all about them. *Lie till you die*, that's their custom. But I don't give a shit because I have this," he lifted a broad sheaf of the gleaming cloth, "and so no matter what they do, I've got mine."

"Why does Grandpa hate gypsies so much?"

"In the old country he was a peaceful farmer, just trying to get along, and had to battle the gypsies constantly. They were wild as hell. They'd rob the farmers, steal their horses. The young men would seduce peasant women. Grandpa said it was terrible the way they'd be up all night dancing and whooping and catting around. He said he was disgusted to watch their goings-on."

"Probably he was jealous," Abel said. To himself he thought, *Right. One of those peaceful farmers who was all smiley and happy as the Nazis were loading the gypsies into the box cars.*

〉〉〉〉

Joe and Abel worked the rest of the morning. As he sewed, Abel's mind returned over and over—*Like a dog to its vomit*, he thought—to bitter fights he and Aaron had had. They were sometimes about Aaron's other boyfriend, but more often the girlfriend.

"You and your goddamn Bi-curious ads. You ought to call yourself Bi-spurious. You're gayer than I am. You just don't want to admit it because it would make your mom mad."

"My girlfriend—"

"Your *girlfriend*? Have you taken a good look at Juliet? She's like a boy with a vagina."

Abel realized that his life was much more peaceful without Aaron. But he didn't want peace.

At one p.m. he said, "I'm starving. Let me run over and get some subs from Coyle's." Coyle's was the deli across the street, and Abel made his suggestion as a grim joke. Joe and Coyle had been feuding for twenty years. It was something about a cat, nobody could remember what. When business was booming at Coyle's, Joe watched from his doorway and suffered, his blood turning black with hate. At such moments, Abel thought of his father as the Lightning King of the Doorway, because he radiated such electric power of outrage. Joe would point to Coyle's deli window stuffed with richness and say, "Look at that disgusting display. It's as though Coyle doesn't know that people are starving." When Abel was a very little boy, he'd believed that world hunger was Coyle's fault.

Now Abel sometimes sneaked over and had one of the great po'boys, stuffed with shrimp and ham. Coyle would chat with him and then say, "Is your dad ready to give it up yet?"

"Not yet. Pop believes in keeping his wounds green."

The father and son worked all afternoon without stopping. As they worked they talked.

"When is that friend of yours, that Aaron, visiting again? Good kid. Kind of an interesting talker. Bet he has the girls after him."

You got that right, Abel thought. The boys too. If you want to know trouble, just fall in love with a curly-haired charmer who drinks too much. Then if you need even more trouble than that, make him think he's bisexual.

The dress glided forward on the shell-like scallops of its hem. Abel sewed sections of the skirt on the machine. Joe pieced the bodice by hand. At one point he stopped, found the tattered picture of the gown, and read the designer's name. "Christian Dior. Paris motherfucker knew what he was doing."

By mid-afternoon, Abel was already tired. Every morning Joe got him up at six a.m., quoting the Szabo family motto which he said went back to medieval times: *Rise early and sharpen your knife.* Abel would ask if, in the absence of ancient enemies he needed to stab at dawn, he could sleep in. Joe always said no.

Now Joe said, "We have to go faster."

"I can't go faster."

"I can."

The phone rang. Cursing, Joe answered it. He listened for about ten seconds, with a black scowl, then shouted, "Get out of my freaking face about the goddamn suit. If you call again I'll cut it up for ass-wipe." He hung up, muttering. "Goddamn Morelli."

"You mean Dom Morelli? Of the New Jersey Morellis? Pop. Maybe you should have been more . . . more . . ."

"You're afraid he's going to send his goons to cut my thumbs off?" Joe smirked. "Oh, Dom's not such a bad guy when you get to know him. Besides, he's grateful to me. He's the ugliest little psycho you ever saw. But when I got my Prince of Wales glen plaid three-piece on him, he looked so cute I almost wanted to date him myself." Joe laughed his harsh honk. After a minute, Abel joined in.

Twilight came down in the late fall afternoon. At five o' clock, Joe turned the lamps on. He went into the little kitchen in back and made tea. Abel could tell by this that his father thought the dress was going well. Joe had just walked back into the front room, teapot in hand, when the shop door opened and a man walked in.

"We're closed," Joe snapped. Then slowly his face turned so purple Abel was afraid his father was having a stroke. The man's parka hood concealed most of his face, so you could see only the flat, expressionless eyes. Abel was trying to make sense of this—and of the man's rank smell where before there had been only the clean odor of fine cloth—when somehow from one second to the next there was a long-barreled gun in that dirty hand.

"Get your money." He spoke in a low flat voice. "Get all of it and get it now, or you're dead." He lifted the gun. Joe, paralyzed, saw the barrel boring into his son's forehead.

I'm going to die, Abel thought, *and I never told Aaron I love him.*

"Did you hear me? Don't fool with me!" Suddenly the thief lifted his filthy boot and kicked over the table on which the dress lay.

"What—the—FUCK!" Joe screamed. He flung the teapot straight into the thief's face. He snatched up his shears, charged forward showing his teeth like a barrel-bellied gorilla, head-butted the man, rammed him flat against a display case with his big paunch, and slashed his parka from shoulder to shoulder. Screams came from the parka hood stained with blood and boiling tea.

"Now get the hell out of here," Joe shouted, "or I'll tell your mom. And leave the goddamn gun here. What were you thinking? I don't have time for your bull."

Abel expected to see a baseball-sized hole bubble up red in his father's chest, but instead the man dropped his gun and staggered out, weeping and babbling to himself like a griefstricken child. Abel stared after him, then opened his stiff lips and said to Joe, "What were you thinking? He was all set to blow my head off—"

"Oh, that was just Mort Peevey's son Davy, the one who was always strange. He did this a few times before. Once I had to stop Grandpa from cutting his liver out. The old guy hauled out a machete I didn't even know he had." Joe looked regretfully at the shattered teapot. "Remember Davy? I'm sorry I broke his nose and ruined his jacket, but somebody has to wake that kid up." He lifted the dress sections and carefully checked them. "I was worried he got his dirt on the dress—"

"Are you crazy? He had a gun to my head!"

"Big deal. Thirty years ago, when Grandpa and I started this shop, I had a gun to my head about every other day. One time Grandpa took a bad hit from a baseball bat, and he still managed to strangle the robber to death with his bare hands."

"That old monster should have been locked up years ago!"

"No, he did right. Some people just belong dead."

"I'm calling 911!"

"We ain't doing that. Davy is Mort and Betty's only kid. It would break their hearts. He's harmless. And besides, we've got to finish the dress."

They argued about it, but in the end, Abel sat down at the sewing machine. It was several minutes before he could still the trembling in his hands enough to sew.

"And I don't like you disrespecting your grandpa like that, calling him a monster," Joe said. He was hand-sewing a complicated buttonhole without looking at it. "He's got reasons. He went through stuff in the war he's never talked about, it was so bad. He got blown up, barely got out with his life. Not everybody has had everything so soft and easy like you've had."

Abel thought, *I lost Aaron because of this crazy obsessed old fucker.* Bitterly he reflected that his father, his grandfather, and every single one of the Szabo forebears he'd ever heard about were the same: swarthy, barrel-chested, raving men charging their demented projects with their tusks, focusing on the desire like blind wild pigs. He thought with painful longing of Aaron's parents. Aaron's father was a Wall Street broker. The worst impropriety he ever committed was to have a third Bloody Mary.

Finally, Abel thought he could trust his voice to stay steady. He said, "When you talked me into coming back here, you said the neighborhood was gentrified."

"It's getting there," Joe said.

"I don't know why we're working so hard," Joe said an hour later. "She'll just tear the dress when she and the groom jump over the incinerator, or run down the chicken for the shaman, or whatever the hell it is they do."

"Irish Travellers are Catholics," Abel said. "She'll be married by a priest."

Joe kept looking at the dress, studying it. He said, "I just don't get it about those women. They could marry anybody. But Grandpa said gypsies marry their cousins, or powerful old men from their tribe. And he said some of these guys would kill you as soon as look at you. Now does it make a bit of frigging sense to you that a woman would marry somebody like that? Because it doesn't to me."

The dress was finished at 6:30. Joe said, "That's it." He hung it up. He arranged the skirt so that it flowed smoothly from the slim calyx of the bodice. He said, "I wonder if she'll like it."

Abel said, "You mean the aunt?" Joe ignored him, got his camera, and took some pictures of the dress.

"You like her," Abel said. "Why don't you go for it, try your moves?"

"So I could be the gypsy king?" Joe said. "Tell it to another fool." He checked the pictures on his camera. "Dating her would be like trying to saddle a wildcat. Marrying her would be like running uphill ten miles with a rabid fox clamped to my arm. *A foreign rabid fox.*"

Good point, Jozsef, Abel thought. *You're going to end up like Grandpa, an old weird Czech guy dying of loneliness, with fur growing on his back. And I'm even dumber than you, because I left the one I love the best.* Aloud he said, "You ought to get out more. You're getting odd."

Joe walked over to the cupboard to put the camera away. "There is nobody for me," he said.

He put on a tweed sports jacket, his best. *Whoop-de-do*, Abel thought. Joe unlocked the front door. He stood at its window, his arms folded. Half an hour passed. At 7:30 he said, "They're probably late because somebody stole a turkey and got shot in the pants."

Abel said nothing, but there flashed through his mind an image of a car wreck, and the women with their fine faces and bright skirts charred in a ball of flame.

At that moment, the Cadillac, like a huge elongated traveling pearl, drew up fast under the street light.

Joe said, "Their lives may be dark, but their Cadillac is as white as snow."

The car door flew open and skirt ruffles flared as the aunt jumped out. She rushed toward the shop. She wore a superb cashmere shawl and amethyst silk suit, but it was all in crazy disarray, uneven and half-buttoned, as though she'd dressed while running for her life from an invading army. She had a bundle on her shoulder.

"My, my, here she comes in a terrible hurry," Joe said softly. "What a surprise. Hold on to your back fillings, Abel."

But they stopped smiling when they saw the woman's face. She was dead white, her mouth trembling. She ran into the shop, not acknowledging them, staring past them. She threw her bundle on the counter and said, "It's the same rug." She seized the wedding dress on its hanger and turned to run out.

Joe grabbed her arm and said, "Just a minute," and then slowly raised his hand to stare at it. It was covered with red. The silk of her sleeve was stained red. "Tell me," he said. She put her mouth to his ear and whispered fiercely.

"I don't understand you," Joe said. His voice sounded funny. "You'll have to show me." The two of them started out the door. Abel was on their heels, and Joe turned around and gripped his son's shoulder hard. "Stay in the shop," he said in a low voice. "I don't know what this is about. I think they've staged something to get us away from the cash register."

But Abel did leave the shop and follow them. He saw Joe wrench open the car door, and as light flooded the dark interior Abel saw two young heads close together, their black hair commingled. Mareid was holding in her arms a young man who was as beautiful a boy as she was a girl, but his formal black suit jacket was wet with red.

Wounded to the death, Abel thought, and then wondered why he'd assumed that. The aunt and Mareid began a fierce argument, Abel did not understand about what. His father bent half inside the car, angry and amused, telling the boy to stop being such a fake. He slapped him lightly, and then threw open the reddened jacket triumphantly, as though to expose a fraud. But anybody could see the deep gash in the kid's side, and that it was seeping blood. After a minute, Joe reached in and touched the cut. Abel was reminded of a picture he'd seen in church of the disciple they called Doubting Thomas, who placed his hands in Christ's wounds before he could believe in them. His father stayed still, hunched over, then straightened up.

"Abel, get some cloth," he said.

"What—"

"Anything, anything," Joe said. Abel ran into the shop and snatched a bundle of material, then rushed back toward the car. The cloth fell open and when the car lights hit it filaments of gold and silver and white flowers flared up on the ghostly white background. Joe grabbed the wedding fabric without comment, formed it into a thick pad, bent again inside the car and pushed the cloth against the boy's side. "Hold that tight," he said to Mareid. "Don't let it slip." Then he said to the aunt, "I'll drive," and they were gone. Abel looked wonderingly down the dark empty street.

Abel waited all night for his father to come back. Around two a.m. the phone rang. He answered it. He could hear Aaron mumbling the way he did when he was drunk. "Oh shit. Shit. Shit. I love you. God damn you to hell for all eternity for leaving me. Oh shit, shit. I'm sorry. God I'm so sorry. Please come back. We can all work it out. Justin and Juliet—"

The wall mirror before Abel glazed crimson when he heard the names spoken. In a frenzy he shouted into the phone that Aaron was throwing fucking *Justin and Juliet* into the street that night, that very minute, and cleansing the apartment of their stupid crap and bongs and ugly weasel asses, that Abel was going to stand there and listen to him do it, and that Abel had better not see them, hear them, or smell them when he came back the next day, and that if Aaron didn't get it done he, Abel, would deal with it himself and would make sure that Aaron regretted it the longest day he ever lived.

Abel was dimly amazed to hear his father's and grandfather's steely voice of rage coming out of him, but mostly he was just furious. He stood there with the receiver to his ear and heard Aaron kick Justin and Juliet out of bed with surprising sobriety, and order them to pack their possessions into trash bags and clear out. They staggered around the apartment screaming. Aaron calmly withstood their wails, curses, desperately offered allurements and threats, and within five minutes had slammed the door after them. There was the sound of steps approaching the phone.

"Now are you happy, Mister Butch Maniac?" Aaron said into his ear.

Abel looked up and saw himself in the wall mirror, a big barrel-chested man sweating and panting, his white teeth snarling in his dark face.

Joe came back at dawn. Abel saw him climb slowly out of a taxi. Joe entered the shop. Abel started to ask questions, but when he saw his father's face, he stopped. Joe walked past him into the little kitchen in back.

"There's blood all over your jacket," Abel said.

Joe put a kettle on the stove and brought out the coffee tin. After a minute he began to talk.

"What happened is that the kid and his friends just thought they'd stop for a quick drink before the wedding. His name is Damon, by the way. They went to the wrong bar. There was a fight, and he was stabbed. His friends got him out of there, bleeding like a pig. They don't believe much in calling the police, but they were going to take him to the Emergency Room. Damon wouldn't let them, said he had to get married first. They tried to force him and he fought them. They called Dolores, that's the aunt, and she and Mareid rushed over and picked him up. He made them come over here to get the dress, said that was how he'd always pictured his bride and that was how it was going to be. The fight Mareid and Dolores had, that was about taking him to the Emergency Room. Mareid wanted to do it right away, but Dolores said they should get married first and then go."

"But why?" Abel said. "Why wait to take him?"

"Because that little girl needed to get married," Joe said, "and that boy needed to marry her, dead or alive." He poured coffee into two mugs. "I knew it when she was standing in the fitting room."

"So you're saying the groom was willing to bleed to death rather than risk that the bride should be an unwed mother."

"They protect their girls." Joe put sugar in his cup, stirred, and set the spoon down. "She's sixteen. He's seventeen."

"Well, did they get married? Were you there?"

"They got married all right. Done and done. I held him up." Joe blew on his coffee, then slowly drank it. "Nice-looking kid, even stabbed in the spleen. And a gutsy kid. Made them take wedding pictures afterward—just head shots, of course. For her to have, he said. Then we went to the Emergency Room."

"What happened there? How is he?"

"So-so. They did an operation. He's alive. That damned old priest Father Karl was there on death watch, hoping for the worst. He's mad now because he wanted to give Damon the Last Rites, and Damon wouldn't let him. Tried to hit the priest. Said he was staying. Hell of a tough kid. Then, when the priest insisted, Mareid went after him with an IV stand. I actually felt sorry for the man. Here he thought he had Damon all squared away, and the kid just refused to stay planted. The priest is not used to people like that."

Abel studied the coffee mug in his hands. "I checked the rug. It's the right one." Joe said nothing. "How did the dress look?"

Joe was silent, the better to savor his memory of Mareid rearing up in the white dress, both dress and girl blazing with beauty, as she brandished the IV stand. Then he said, "It looked good." He finished his coffee and put the cup down.

He was turning to go when Abel said, "Pop." Joe stopped. "Pop, I'm gay."

Joe said, "I know."

"I'm going back to Aaron tomorrow."

Joe sighed heavily and looked down, so Abel wouldn't see in his eyes what he saw: his grandchildren running out of the shop. He remembered with shame that he'd planned to talk Abel into naming his first son Dano, after Grandpa. The delusions of a fool. He said, "I had the most beautiful piece of wool you ever saw put aside for your wedding suit." He continued to look down, stubbornly seeing his son in the suit.

"I'll still need it. Marriage between guys is legal in Massachusetts."

"So I got that to look forward to," Joe said.

"Aaron and I—"

"You're the last of the Szabos."

"Why is it all on me? You could get married again. Hell, Grandpa could marry his nurse and breed like a rabbit." Joe swore, but Abel thought he could see a smile there. He could also see Joe wasn't done.

"There—there are . . . I mean, they got—ah—like, different roles—like, there's you, and there's Aaron—"

It took Abel a minute, but he finally had it. The old freak thought that in gay couples there was always a husband and a wife. And he'd feel a little bit better if his son was the husband.

"It's none of your frigging business," Abel said.

In the front room, Joe stood at the window and looked out, his arms folded. The neighborhood was already drenched in pink. He remembered the thing that had happened at the hospital that he had not told Abel about. He thought he would probably never tell him.

The doctors had been operating on Damon. Dolores and Mareid insisted on standing in the hall outside the operating room, so he stood with them. After an hour, Mareid fainted. He caught her, and he and Dolores carried her to the waiting room. He got juice and sandwiches for her from the cafeteria as Dolores fanned her. He held the orange juice to Mareid's lips and concentrated on feeding it to her drop by drop, like a baby.

Dolores watched Joe. After a few minutes she said, "We'd heard you were a fine tailor. But we chose you because you're Dano Szabo's son. We have Czech friends who told us about him. About how bad he was when he was young, stabbed his brother in the back, ran off with his wife. Lived like a beast, all the other gypsies despised him. Then during the war this criminal, this disgrace—I'm sorry," she said to Joe, but he shook his head, "—he got brave. Blew up train tracks and rescued our people out of the box cars. Kept them alive in the mountains. Dano Szabo! I thought his son would have good energy for us. I was not wrong."

Joe knew he was gaping like a dumb brute. He couldn't think of a word to say. But after a minute, he began to plan a conversation he would have with Grandpa Szabo, as soon as possible, in the nursing home.

Now, across the street, lights went on in Coyle's deli. In its window hung a big mortadella and smoked turkey. There was a carved ham, and Joe could see how pink the slices were under the browned crust of fat, spilling over a blue platter. There were pineapples, and piles of round seeded buns, cheeses, and baskets of grapes, peaches, and apples. There were white chrysanthemums in a yellow bowl. Coyle could make a nice window, he had to admit it.

Little Coyle was sweeping the sidewalk in front of his store. Joe opened his own door, stepped outside and began walking across the street. Coyle stared at him, took in the bloody jacket and hastily went inside. Joe smiled to himself.

He stood in front of the deli window and considered it, his hands on his hips. Inside, he could see Coyle watching him nervously, big-eyed like a bunny in headlights. Joe nodded to him coolly. Then he turned back to the sliced ham and big brown rolls. He began to plan the food he would take to the hospital. The family shouldn't have to eat that cafeteria crap.

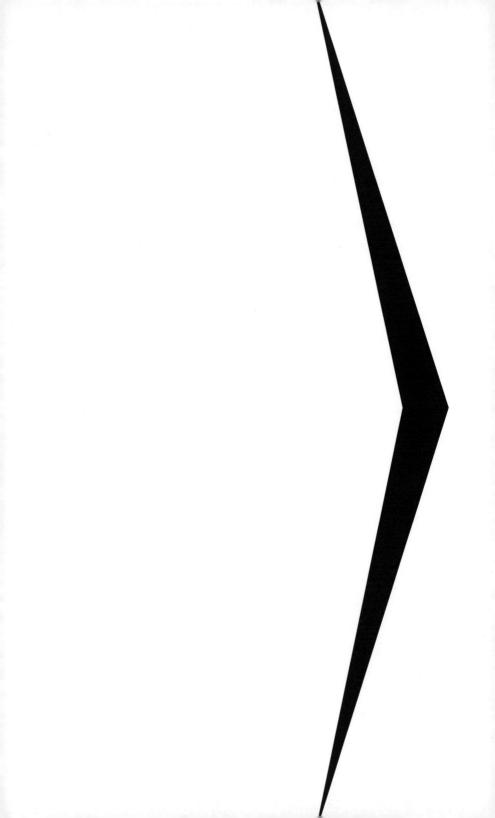

ACKNOWLEDGEMENTS

The following publications have published previous versions of these stories, some in different forms:

The Antioch Review: "In The Midnight Hour" Fall 1985, Volume 43, Number 4.
"Simeon and Johanna" Spring 2013, Volume 71, Number 2.
"Joe Szabo and the Gypsy Bride" Winter 2014, Volume 72, Number 1.

Barnstorm, Contemporary Wisconsin Fiction: "Egyptian" The University of Wisconsin Press, Terrace Books, 2005.

The Georgia Review 11: "Gabriel Desperado" Winter 1997, Volume LI, Number 4 and reprinted in The Georgia Review retrospective issue, Selected Stories and Art, 1984-2007, Volume LXV, Number 1, both under original title, "Angela Perfidia."

Main Street Rag: "The Wanderer" *The Book of Villains* anthology, September 2011.
"Maera's Day" Fall 2014, Volume 19, Number 4.

The Rake: "Party Doll" October 2006 magazine issue.

Rosebud: "Simeon Prophet" August 2008, Issue 42.
"Y Nosotros Debemos, Aye, Morir" Autumn 2011, Issue 51.

Wisconsin Academy Review: "Prizes" Summer 2005 issue.

Wisconsin Fiction, Wisconsin Sesquicentennial issue: "Marrying Jerry" University of Wisconsin Press, Volume 85, 1997.

Zoetrope: All-Story: "Boy Into Panther" Summer 1999, Volume 3, Number 2.

ABOUT THE AUTHOR

Margaret Benbow's stories have appeared in many magazines and anthologies. She's won numerous awards for both stories and poems. Benbow received Pushcart nominations, an Arts Board grant, Library Association award, the Paula Chandler Prize, the Walt McDonald First Book Award for a poetry collection, Zona Gale Award, and many others. Most recently, she received the New Rivers Many Voices Project prize for fiction. She's now writing a novel in linked stories about outsider artists, whom she admires very much: their struggles, loves, enemies, incredible persistence, and occasional startling triumphs against all odds.

ABOUT NEW RIVERS PRESS

New Rivers Press emerged from a drafty Massachusetts barn in winter 1968. Intent on publishing work by new and emerging poets, founder C.W. "Bill" Truesdale labored for weeks over an old Chandler & Price letterpress to publish three hundred fifty copies of Margaret Randall's collection *So Many Rooms Has a House but One Roof.*

About four-hundred titles later, New Rivers, a nonprofit and now learning press, based since 2001 at Minnesota State University Moorhead, has remained trued to Bill's goal of publishing the best new literature—poetry and prose—from new, emerging, and established writers.

As a learning press, New Rivers guides student editors, designers, writers, and filmmakers through the various processes involved in selecting, editing, designing, publishing, and distributing literary books. In working, learning, and interning with New Rivers Press, students gain integral real-world knowledge that they bring with them into the publishing workforce at positions with publishers across the country, or to begin their own small presses and literary magazines.

New Rivers Press authors range in age from twenty to eighty-nine. They include a silversmith, a carpenter, a geneticist, a monk, a tree-trimmer, and a rock musician. They hail from cities such as Christchurch, Honolulu, New Orleans, New York City, Northfield (Minnesota), and Prague.

Charles Baxter, one of the first authors with New Rivers calls the press "the hidden backbone of the American literary tradition." Continuing this tradition, in 1981 New Rivers began to sponsor the Minnesota Voices Project (now called Many Voices Project) competition. It is one of the oldest literary competitions in the United States, bringing recognition and attention to emerging writers. Other New Rivers publications include the American Fiction Series, the

American Poetry Series, New Rivers Abroad, and the Electronic Book Series.

Please visit our website: *newriverspress.com* for more information.

MANY VOICES PROJECT
AWARD WINNERS

("OP" indicates that the paper copy is out of print; "e-book" indicates that the title is available as an electronic publication.)